REVELATIONS

Lady C. Investigates

Book Two

Issy Brooke

CHAPTER ONE

The ponderous thud of the long-case clock seemed to be marking off each second in the slow shuffle towards death. Cordelia, Lady Cornbook sipped at her tea and grimaced as cold black leaves touched her tongue.

Nothing stayed hot for long in this draughty, rambling Tudor house. She couldn't physically wear any more layers of clothing and yet still retain movement of her limbs. She tried to lean closer to the small fire in the grate. It was a very special type of fire; one that seemed to cast out no heat whatsoever. Just angry sparks that would smoulder, unnoticed, in the folds of one's skirts until the smell told you it was too late to stop a hole appearing in the fabric.

"Isn't this marvellous!" trilled her maiden aunt, Maude Stanbury. "I am so very glad that you are here, my dear Cordelia. And are you sure I cannot tempt you to stay for Christmas? Two weeks hardly seems long enough after the journey you have endured to reach me here."

"Thank you, but no. I really do want to be back at my house, now it is officially mine."

Maude's toothless mouth worked, her flaccid cheeks blowing like bellows. It was an unconscious habit of hers that she made as she sank deep into thought, and Cordelia was starting to find it hypnotic. She knew that Maude was trying to find a socially acceptable way of saying "You cannot stay a widow forever. You should have married that Hugo Hawke fellow and be done with it."

Before Maude could voice her objection, Cordelia said, "I must say, I am looking forward to some of the festive soirees and balls that are planned, and I thank you kindly for the invitations, but I don't want to miss out on preparing my own house for the winter season, too."

"You are welcome to stay for as long as you wish," Maude assured her.

In truth, she had only been at Four Trees on the North Yorkshire Moors for three days so far, and it had already been a feat of endurance for Cordelia. She would have hurled herself back into her travelling chariot the very same day that she arrived, if she could have done so without seeming rude. The house was hewn of grey stone and appeared to emerge like a rocky grey outcrop from the side of the grey hill. The sky had remained dark grey and even when she'd caught a glimpse of the sun, it too had been pale grey and masked by grey clouds.

And there were no trees at Four Trees.

The ticking of the clock seemed to be slowing down the more that Cordelia listened to it. She replaced her cup on her china saucer, and the clatter echoed around the low-ceilinged sitting room. Her fingers twitched. She had read all of the books she had brought with her. She had talked of all the socially appropriate things that she could talk of with Maude. At this rate, she'd be taking up embroidery and that could only end in stabbings and tears.

When someone knocked at the door, Cordelia nearly whooped with joy. *At last! An interruption!* She didn't care what it might be. Anything short of violence would be welcome.

Maude's staff were few. There was a cook who lived in, a daily girl who came in from the town, and Maude's companion, the sullen and porcelain-faced Lizzie McNab. When Cordelia had turned up with her own maid and her coach boy Stanley, they had almost doubled the household.

It was Lizzie who opened the door and peered in. Cordelia couldn't help but wonder if her shockingly white face was due to the extreme cold, an artful use of powder, or whether it was a natural pallor. She was from an impoverished gentle family and looked on everything and

7

everyone with a supercilious and glassy stare.

"Madam, my lady," she whispered huskily. Her voice belonged to a Parisian brothel-keeper, not a well-to-do young lady. "Madam, there is a family here to see you. But they are from the town."

"Oh. To see me? On what matter?" Maude said, looking confused. The town was around a mile away, the other side of the church, along a rough track. Rain sleeted against the windows. No one would be abroad in the grey storm if they could help it.

"I know not." Lizzie shrugged. "There is a man, his slatternly wife, and some ragged boy."

"Go and find out," Maude said, getting slowly to her feet. Cordelia rushed to her side to help her find her balance. "Are they in the hall?"

"No, madam. I've left them on the doorstep."

In anyone else, Cordelia would have taken that for sarcasm but she had learned enough of Lizzie's snobbery and spite to know she spoke the truth. Maude gripped Cordelia's arm and sighed.

"Bring them into the hallway and I shall speak to them there."

Lizzie's eyelids flickered closed but not quickly enough to prevent Cordelia seeing the companion had rolled her eyes. She disappeared.

Cordelia brought Maude along, walking slowly behind.

* * *

By the time that Cordelia and Maude had wound their way through various dank corridors and reached the dark hallway, Lizzie had brought the trio inside. It was still bitterly cold but at least they were no longer being rained upon. They clustered by the door, wrapped in as many grey and brown blankets and rags as they could find, their skeletal hands clutching at the edges of their garments to hold them closed over their shivering bodies.

The hall had once been the main room of the house, but was now an open cavern, empty and silent. It wasn't even lit but Lizzie darted off to the kitchen and returned with a lamp. She held it near Maude, clearly not wishing to get too close to the family.

The boy coughed, and Cordelia spoke sharply. It wasn't her house or her place, but she said, "We must take these people through to the sitting room. At least they might be warm there."

Maude's cheeks quivered. "Ah—"

"Nay, we shan't stay long," the man said, shooting a black look up at them. He was holding his wet cloth cap between his hands, and his body was in a deferential pose. But his voice was harsh, in spite of the long northern vowels, and his eyes glittered from their deep setting below

9

the jutting ridge of his forehead. "We come only to say that our boy needs his position back, madam."

"He has no position here. Why, I do not even know you," Maude said.

"He and I, we work at Stoney Mill," the man said. "Or at least, our lad did until he was laid off last week for the winter."

"Then that is a matter for my brother-in-law. You must speak to Mr Welsh, not me. I am sorry. Lizzie, take them to the kitchens. Tell cook she can give them soup and bread, and something to take away with them as well."

"Nay," said the man, shaking his head. "We have seen Mr Welsh and he said there is nothing to be done when the work drops off for winter, but we cannot have that. Do you think to starve us?"

"Not I," said Maude. "But I am sure that there is always something for a hard-working, God-fearing person. You said you were in employment. And your wife?"

"She does work, also. But our lad … we need it, madam. The price of bread rises and we cannot work any harder than we do. We aren't asking for charity, only the chance of hard work."

"I do not know how many workers my brother-in-law has laid off for the winter, but rest assured that we do not do it lightly. And if he were to keep everyone on, why then, wages should have to be cut. Would you accept that? I think not. So, then, let your boy attend some school this winter and he will return to work in the spring a better person for a little learning. Lizzie – to the kitchens, please. Good day."

Maude's hand tightened on Cordelia's arm and she shuffled around, heading slowly back to the corridor that led to the warm — relatively speaking — sitting room. Cordelia had to turn with her, but she glanced back.

The man was staring at them with malice etched into every line of his weather-beaten face. His wife was not much better. She bared her teeth at Cordelia. The boy simply stared at the floor, and his bare hands were shaking.

"Come on, then," Lizzie snapped, and opened the door that led to the kitchen.

"Cordelia, let us get back to the fire," Maude urged, and Cordelia turned away from the unnerving tableau.

* * *

Cordelia counted the ticks of the clock for ten whole minutes, before declaring she had a headache and retiring to her room. Maude was concerned, but Cordelia assured her that if she took a nap, she would be refreshed for dinner.

She was pleased to find that her maid, Ruby, had lit a small fire in the grate in the bedroom. The room was long and rather narrow, and Ruby's bed had been set up at the far end, behind a screen and a wardrobe. Cordelia's bed was at the other end, and in the centre stood some armchairs and a table.

There were three sets of narrow, mullioned windows along the outside wall, showing nothing but greyness beyond.

"You look half-frozen," Ruby chided, dragging one of the chairs closer to the fire and urging Cordelia to sit.

Cordelia sat for less than half a minute before launching to her feet again. She took to pacing up and down. "I know I should stay for a week," she said, "but goodness me, it is wearing. Maude does nothing but sit and stare into the fire. There are some parties coming up, and little country gatherings, but I think I shall be dead in a puddle of boredom by the time anything happens. How do you fare?"

Ruby took the seat that she had pulled to the fire for Cordelia, and sighed. "Much the same, I fear," she said. "Oh, what possessed you to come here?"

"She has been pressing me for some time. I suppose she is lonely. I don't imagine many people visit her."

"And now you know why."

"True. And as for that companion of hers, Lizzie…"

"What of her, my lady?" Ruby said, cocking her head back and levelling a direct stare at her mistress. Her tone changed instantly, losing the light air and becoming flat.

"Oho," said Cordelia, with a smile. The two young women were of a similar age, after all. "You have become friends with her, have you?"

Ruby shrugged. "We have talked. She hasn't had anyone else to talk to. She's been here for over a year now, and feels quite abandoned by her family. She has older brothers and sisters, you know, all married, and not one of them feels they can offer her a home. They don't even write."

"She gives the impression that any hard work or service is beneath her."

"Maybe it is."

"Work is beneath no one," Cordelia said. "Why, even I work."

Ruby laughed. "Oh, this infernal cookery book of yours!" She hastily added, "Of course, it will take much work, my lady. Did you not say that you were to talk to people here about their regional food?"

"I hoped I might. Unfortunately, my darling aunt Maude has poured scorn on all my feeble plans, and refuses to introduce me to anyone useful. I did attempt to speak to her cook but she went numb with fear and dribbled a bit. I feared for the pastry, and withdrew."

"So, that is that?"

"For the moment. But I still harbour my plans to

explore British food and maybe write in a magazine about it, and collect the articles in a small book. There are others doing similar."

"How would yours be different, then?"

Cordelia stopped by the central window and peered through the thick, wavy glass. "Oh, I don't know. It would simply be better."

Ruby snickered under her breath. Cordelia was about to remonstrate with her, although she knew that they were both sinking into bickering out of sheer boredom, when her attention was caught by a dark figure coming down the track towards the house.

"A hooded woman approaches," Cordelia said. "More plaintiffs from the mill, perhaps?"

"What has happened at the mill?" Ruby asked as she came to Cordelia's side.

"Some of the younger workers are laid off for the winter, that's all," Cordelia said. "One family came earlier to beg for work."

"No," Ruby said, peering through the window. "That's only Iris." She went back to the fireside and poked at the coals.

"Iris? She's still here?"

"As you see, yes. Maude is never satisfied with the cut of her gown. If Iris does not put her foot down, she will be here for a year."

"Poor girl." Cordelia watched until the woman had entered the house and disappeared from view. "What a life that must be. Travelling from house to house, attending to people's clothing, at their beck and call, never being part of any household."

"At some point she'll meet a man and that will be the end of her seamstressing. I suppose then she'll take in mending and have children and so it goes."

"She keeps herself very close," Cordelia said. "I never see her about the house."

"She is full of secrets," Ruby said. "Alas, none of them are terribly interesting. She doesn't talk when we eat together in the servants' hall, such as it is. She shares a room presently with Lizzie, and those two do not rub along well together."

"I should imagine not," Cordelia said, thinking of Lizzie's haughtiness and Iris's mousey demeanour. "Why do they share?"

"Warmth, I'd imagine," Ruby said, poking the fire pointedly.

She had a point. There were many rooms in the manor house but most lay unused, like dusty icehouses. Cordelia sighed. "Is it time to dress for dinner yet?"

"Only two hours more, my lady."

Cordelia uttered a bad word she'd heard from her coachman, and Ruby smiled.

CHAPTER TWO

"I rather fear I would burst into flames the minute I stepped over the threshold," Ruby said. "I've not attended a service for many years."

"I think that Maude does expect us all to attend church with her today," Cordelia replied. She glanced out of the bedroom window. "Look. It's not raining … at the moment. A walk would be just the thing."

"Well, I know that Lizzie does not go, and nor does Iris. I don't see why she would expect me."

"Please come," Cordelia urged. "Do it for me. And yourself. Why, are you not turning a little strange from being closeted here for four days now?"

"This visit was your idea."

"This was my *command*," Cordelia pointed out, using her Mistress Voice.

Ruby sighed, but she flounced her way to the travelling

chest to dig out some suitable outdoor footwear. "What about Stanley? This is more his sort of thing."

"Indeed, and he is driving Maude to the church in her Brougham." Cordelia shook her head. The carriage was pulled by two horses and seemed an unnecessary extravagance for a short journey on a rough country lane; a gig or dogcart would have sufficed, and indeed there was a gig in her stables. But Maude had said she had standards to maintain. It was Sunday: she would ride in her carriage.

"What sort of church are we going to?" Ruby asked. "Will there be shouting and brimstone?"

"Perhaps," Cordelia said, "but I shall try not to." She smiled wickedly.

* * *

No. It was not the sort of church where any shouting was likely to happen under the vaulted arches. The dust kept everything silent. Even the hymns were muttered in a hushed, toneless drone. It was a traditional Established kind of place, thoroughly Church of England. Maude met Cordelia at the lych-gate, and led her to the front where a pew was slightly elevated for the better sort of parishioner. Simeon Welsh, her brother-in-law, was already seated. He rose to greet them.

Stanley took a seat automatically at the back. Ruby, likewise, was sent to the narrower pews with the rest of the hoi-polloi. She slitted her eyes at Cordelia, who was rather taken aback at the strict demarcation between the wealthy patrons and the common herd. *Country ways*, she thought to herself. *I don't like this. I know it's been the same in some big city churches but for some reason I thought it would be more egalitarian here.*

Simeon Welsh was a finely dressed man of middling years with more of the "city dandy" written all over him than the "country squire" she had first expected when she met him at dinner the night she arrived. Even here in church he was a fine sight, from his ebony cane to his checked shirt and royal blue jacket. Where other people were dressed soberly for the service, he was a vision in clashing modern colours and patterns. He smiled warmly, and ushered Maude and Cordelia onto the pew. He resumed his seat once they were settled, so that Cordelia was wedged between Maude and Simeon.

"And how do you do, Lady Cornbrook?" he asked as he got himself comfortable again.

"Very well, thank you. Do call me Cordelia. We are family."

"Of course," he said. "I should be honoured."

What was the correct title for one's aunt's late sister's widowed husband? She thought. She resolved to consult Debrett's *Peerage & Baronetage* at the earliest opportunity.

They made polite small talk for a short time — the weather, the state of the track, the pleasant walk — until the tallest, thinnest Reverend in the country ascended the pulpit and began to whisper something which may, or may not, have been about pears. Or maybe bears.

Cordelia resorted to biting the inside of her cheek to stay alert, although she could tell from the light snoring in the pews behind her that not everyone felt that same compunction. The Reverend was as grey as the hills and the stones in both appearance and passion. Even though the front pew was not so far from the pulpit, his words wavered in and out of earshot.

All things must end, she repeated to herself until finally the Reverend clambered down from the pulpit and shuffled to the door. By slow degrees, the congregation woke up, stretched, and began to make their way outside, blinking in the harsh winter light cast from a strangely brilliant low sun.

Simeon moved to one side to talk to a man dressed as a well-fed tradesperson, and Cordelia took Maude's arm to bring her to the Reverend. He stood in the porch, shaking the hands of his parishioners and murmuring a few words to each as they passed him to thank him.

Maude introduced Cordelia to the Reverend, whose handshake was exactly as damp and weak as she had imagined. His eyes, however, were hard and keen and she was surprised to be pinned by his gaze.

"What did you make of my lesson today?" he asked in a whispery voice.

She could hardly lie. "I confess I found parts of it hard to follow."

He took it to mean that she hadn't understood it, rather than hadn't heard it, which was what she intended. *I may as well hide behind the usual perception of feminine shortcomings*, she thought, and smiled.

He was about to say something else when everyone's attention was caught by an altercation on the track outside the boundary wall of the churchyard.

Cordelia and Maude began to move towards the noise, but as soon as Cordelia laid her eyes on the man who was currently shouting, she stopped. Maude pressed against her. "What is it, my dear?"

"Who is he?" she said in a low voice. The man's energy and vitality crackled from him as he waved his fist in the air, his head thrown back at an angle as he preached to the very sky.

The Reverend came to Cordelia's other side. "That man there is one of society's great evils," he muttered. "A seditious sort, bent upon undermining all that is good and true."

"Goodness me."

The man was tall, with wide square shoulders which tapered to a narrow, lean body. He wore a black jacket cut in a working man's style, squared off just below the hips, and a hat that was not tall enough to be a topper but too large to be anything else. As they watched, he scrambled up like an acrobat onto the stone wall, and began to wave a sheaf of papers in the air. He turned slowly so that he was facing the crowd now gathered in the churchyard.

His eyes, set wide in his swarthy outdoor face, *burned*. Unlike the meek Reverend, his voice was loud and clear and stroked a finger of flame along Cordelia's spine; it was a rich, deep voice.

"There is no political good to be achieved by a spirit of exclusiveness!" he cried. "In some places, I hear, the police have been called to prevent our meetings in public halls — public, I tell you, for the good of all — yet we labour under tyranny and despotism as the rich desperately cling to power, and I say, this is to the detriment of all!"

Some people pushed forward, craning their necks to peer up at the firebrand. Others grabbed their children and hurried them away, putting their hands over the young people's ears.

The man pointed at a mother who was hauling her boy away. "It is for *him* that I work, and for you, goodwife, also. For everyone, the working man, the common man — our strength runs the mills and the machines and the engines — yet our complicity keeps us down! Here, in my pamphlet, we explain what must change, what must change *now* in England to bring about a new revolution, a glorious future, a—"

A stone was thrown, and caught the speaker on his cheek. He put his hand up and touched the trickle of blood.

"You are your own jailers!" he shouted.

"Well, I don't think that's the way to get the listener to feel sympathy for the cause," Cordelia said. "Insulting his very audience won't get him very far."

Maude tightened her grip. "Come, my dear, we must be away."

People were surging to gather around the man on the wall. Some people were shouting, and there seemed to be a mix of opinions. "Hear the man, let him speak," one man called, to be answered by, "Transport them all, Chartists and dissenters and rebels and traitors."

Ruby appeared, elbowing her way through the crowd that was blocking the way to the gate. "My lady, madam, Stanley is waiting with the carriage."

With Ruby on one side, and Cordelia on the other, they cleared a path for Maude, to where Stanley waited with the carriage. His face was drawn and anxious as he listened to the rantings of the man.

"How c-can he be allowed t-to speak so?" the young man muttered as he dropped the step to help Maude into the carriage.

Cordelia knew he was stammering to himself, but she answered him anyway. "Do you not think that every man should have freedom of conscience?"

He blushed and looked down, shaking his head. He found it hard to speak out, but anything to do with religion would compel him to answer, if somewhat awkwardly. "We must obey God, not set ourselves up trying to change the ways and laws of our land," he said with his customary stammer, making his words sound with less conviction than Cordelia knew he felt. "It is as it is designated. Do you ride home in the carriage, my lady?"

"No, thank you."

He closed the door and nodded.

"Ruby?" Cordelia called the maid to her side. "Let us walk back to Four Trees."

Ruby was clutching a sheet of beige paper in her hands. "At once, my lady."

"You have one of the man's pamphlets? Do you agree with his words?" Cordelia asked as they began the stroll along the track. The carriage rumbled ahead, not a great deal faster than their walking pace, but it moved into the distance by slow and inevitable degrees.

"I don't know if I agree yet, my lady," Ruby said, glancing at the pamphlet in her hands. "But I will read it and report back to you anon."

* * *

They walked back briskly to stay warm, although it was pleasant enough in the sunlight. The wind was picking up and when they were in the shade, it was bitingly cold. Ruby folded the pamphlet up and tucked it into her small bag.

Cordelia said, "I am guessing that you slept through the sermon."

"A little, but I was watching people, mostly," Ruby said. "Wasn't it dull? I am sure Stanley enjoyed it. Please tell me, my lady, that we shall have left to return to Clarfields before next Sunday. I don't think I wish to go again."

"I think you're right," Cordelia said. "I can't sit through that again. Maybe we can cut short our visit, and leave around Wednesday, I think. A week would be sufficient for politeness' sake…"

Ruby groaned. "Three more days! And you know that it shall drag on and on today. Sundays are the very worst of days."

"They are supposed to be the best of days," Cordelia said.

"You should ask Iris that. I shouldn't think she would agree."

Cordelia was about to question Ruby, but there was a figure running down the track towards them. It was Stanley, red-faced and blowing hard. Behind him, they could see that the courtyard in front of Four Trees was alive with activity.

"My lady!" he gasped, and bent double to put his hands on his knees while he caught his breath.

"What is it? What has happened? Is my aunt all right?" Cordelia said, scanning the scene anxiously as she imagined dire carriage accidents.

"Not Mrs Stanbury," Stanley stammered. "The companion, Lizzie McNab. They've found her dead body on the moors at the Ally Cross."

CHAPTER THREE

"I did not care for that parish constable," Cordelia said at breakfast the next morning. "I saw Mr Gold, the magistrate or whatever he is, at a distance, but it was that constable who spoke with me. He … was somewhat *loud*." In truth, she had been quite shocked when the man had arrived at Four Trees, clearly drunk and most unpleasant in both his odour and his manner of speaking.

Maude picked delicately at her eggs and haddock. "Kennett is a boozed old sot, my dear. You must ignore anything that he said to you. What a business, eh? I'm glad it's all over now."

"But it is not over, not remotely," Cordelia said in shock.

Maude did not even look up. They were alone in the dining room, but for Maude's daily girl, Kate, who did the office of serving at meal times, usually assisted by Lizzie.

She was an over-worked girl who had been ordered by Maude, that morning, to stay on and live in now that her companion had gone. Kate usually attended the house for only six and a half days of the week, taking Sunday afternoons off. Now Maude had instructed her to be the Maid-of-All-Work, and reside in the house so she might be at Maude's constant beck and call.

It was cold, as usual. The fire was freshly lit and had not permeated the thick stone walls yet. Cordelia persisted in her conversation, saying, "The poor girl was found dead! There will be an investigation, surely. The constable will talk to everyone here, and the magistrate will want to discover the truth."

"Oh, my dear. I heard all about your escapades at Wallerton Manor. It was such an unfortunate turn of events, most unbecoming. You must not let this put you off your visit here. Forget about that girl. People die all the time on the moors. How are your eggs?"

"Tasteless," Cordelia muttered.

"I shall have Cook spoken to at once," Maude said.

"No, I did not mean that. They are excellent eggs. I simply meant to say that I do not feel much like eating them."

"You are too sensitive," Maude said. "You must learn to put your emotions aside. Men don't like it."

And you would know this how, exactly, Cordelia thought. She sipped at her tea. "Did she die of exposure? Where is the Ally Cross? What did she do up there?"

Maude dropped her heavy silver fork with a resounding clatter onto her plate. She looked up at last. "Cordelia! This is *not appropriate* talk for a meal table. Or for a lady. Or for any situation in which you find yourself."

"Then I am in the wrong situation," Cordelia said. She stood up and put her cutlery neatly on the still-full plate. "Do excuse me."

She was sure that Maude muttered "flighty girl" as she left the room. Cordelia was in her mid-thirties but to Maude she was obviously a silly little thing who simply needed firm direction.

She said as much to Ruby, angrily, as she stamped into the bedroom.

Ruby was curled by the fire there, reading something.

"My lady, she doesn't know you."

"That much is apparent. And I don't know her, and the more that I do know, the less I want to know."

"Er…" Ruby put the paper down and grimaced as she puzzled out her mistress' words. "Well, yes."

"Come along, Ruby, on your feet. We shall pack our things. I cannot stay here a single moment longer. No, I shan't even stay until Wednesday. We are to begin our journey home *today*. I will tell her as we leave. Ha!"

"Oh, good." Ruby swung her legs to the rug and sat forward, but stopped. "My lady; what of Lizzie?"

"What of her?"

"Now *you* are sounding like Maude."

Cordelia put her hands on her hips. "Do not you dare say that."

"I saw that constable yesterday. Didn't you? He got me in a corner. He touched my hips and licked his lips. I told him that he might remove his hand immediately."

"Or?"

Ruby smiled slightly. "Or I would push a hatpin up his nose. A long one."

"Lovely. Well done. Yes, I did see him. To me, he was curt, but at least he kept his hands to himself."

"I wager he would not, if he came upon you alone," Ruby said. "He will not investigate Lizzie's death. Anyway, Maude told him to leave. She said that no one was to talk to anyone in this house about the death. She said it was done, it was over, and that was that. She has had to be persuaded to write word to Lizzie's family, according to Kate. She does not think that anyone will care to bring a prosecution."

"How callous."

"Would you write to a dog's litter-mates if that dog

died?" Ruby said.

"I am shocked at that insinuation," Cordelia said, but even as she did so, she had to acknowledge that Ruby was correct. Maude saw those of inferior status as nothing more than useful domestic animals.

"I know that Lizzie was as much of a snob, in her own way, as Maude was," Ruby said. She chewed her lip and looked into the fire. "But it doesn't seem right to leave it at that. I want to go home; you know I do. But if we do go, no one will do anything about it."

"Who's to say there is anything to be done?" Cordelia said. She knew that she wanted to be persuaded to stay — indeed, in her own head, she was single-handedly bringing a highway robber to justice, somehow — but she wanted to hear Ruby's arguments.

"Of course there is something to be done," Ruby said. "She was found dead up on the lonely moor."

"What do you know that I don't?" Cordelia said. She pulled the other armchair close to the fire and sat down. "How did she die? Was it not exposure to the elements? That is what they want everyone to believe."

"Wouldn't that be easy? No, it was not the cold that killed her, so the general gossip goes. She was well-wrapped in her skirts and shawl and a blanket too. They said that her eyes were open and her pupils but tiny pin-pricks."

"Opium, then!" Cordelia said. "What a foolish girl."

"My lady," Ruby said scornfully. "What opium-eater or laudanum user would take their medicine and then walk out to the moors? The Ally Cross is two miles hence. It is a stone that marks the highest point of a flag-stone path that crosses the moor. They call it a packhorse route. They used to take coffins that way. I know this because … Lizzie had spoken of it."

Cordelia nodded. Of course, Lizzie and Ruby would have conversed, though she couldn't imagine how the packhorse route would have entered conversation. "Have you been there?" she asked.

Ruby shook her head. "No, it is a tough walk in the bad weather."

"It must have been a journey she did not undertake lightly." Cordelia glanced up at the windows. "As soon as it stops raining, we will explore. So, why was she there?"

"She might have walked out there to take the substance."

"Might she?" Ruby sounded supercilious in her doubt. "Such a distance?"

"No, you are right. Perhaps it was not morphia which killed her, then. What else did they say of how she looked?"

Ruby twisted her fingers together as she sought to be accurate in her recount. "They said — those who found her — that there could have been a struggle; that her body was rigid, but that might have been rigor mortis. They weren't sure. She was laid out on the floor, too, not sitting against the stone. That in particular sounds strange to me."

"Indeed it does." Cordelia sat back and they both lapsed into silence for some minutes.

Cordelia was mulling it over. It was not right that Maude was ignoring the death. It was not right that the constable was a drunkard and a fool.

It was not right, therefore, that Cordelia should leave. She had a duty to see justice done, if no one else would.

Eventually, Ruby spoke. "I know you, my lady, and you'll not let this lie."

"Why," she replied with a smile, "anyone would think you are encouraging me in this matter."

"Yes, I am." Ruby grinned. "But I think that you need no encouragement, do you?"

"Perhaps not."

"Do it for me," Ruby said, "as well as for Lizzie. She was a woman like me, you know, in some ways. If I met that fate, who would look into the manner of my death? I need to know that someone would."

Cordelia swallowed. "Of course I would."

"And to know that someone would, well, my lady, that means something."

"Oh," Cordelia said suddenly. "There is a problem. I've argued with Maude. I have been rather rude."

"Is it time for you to eat some humble pie?"

"It is. Ugh."

"Remember the reason and the rest will be easy," Ruby said, sounding like Cordelia herself when she was giving advice.

"Since when did you get so wise?" Cordelia sighed and got to her feet. "Tell me, then. What should I say is my reason for staying on, after I have been so impolite to her?"

"You're writing a book, are you not?"

"She does not like that idea," Cordelia pointed out.

"Have you any ideas that she does like?"

"No. Oh, I wish the others were here."

Ruby raised one eyebrow, and Cordelia turned away. She didn't mean Mrs Unsworth, of course; she referred only to Geoffrey, her dour and protective coachman.

For if things were to involve rambling about the lonely wastelands of Yorkshire, prey to any footpad or hellhound that might be abroad, she knew exactly who she wanted at her side.

It was a shame that she had sent him away.

CHAPTER FOUR

Eating humble pie was very, very hard.

Cordelia thought she'd left all that behind her. Her marriage to the late Sir Cornbrook had been mercifully brief. She had never expected to get married, and it was clear that he had chosen her as his second wife for her *lack* of looks. She knew, as soon as the confetti had cleared, that he assumed that the stocky, solid twenty-seven-year-old Cordelia would turn a blind eye to his dalliances and affairs.

She could not turn away from his brutality and physical chastisements, however. Living in his house became a fear-edged game of cat and mouse, and she had learned to quail and cower.

She stopped her reminiscences before they led on to the manner of his death. That was a locked room she was not going to open. She shook herself and pulled her fringed shawl more tightly around her shoulders. She was in the sitting room, sitting opposite Maude who was in her customary armchair by the feeble fire. Cordelia had finished her inelegant apology and explanation, and now Maude was watching Cordelia closely.

"There is something else, is there not?" Maude said. "You are welcome to stay for as long as you like, of course. I've said as much before. Two weeks is hardly long enough. Stay for Christmas! But at breakfast you made it plain you could not stay, and now you are begging leave to remain."

"My … research."

Maude blew out her cheeks like two small balls. "That book, what nonsense. It's mere piffle, my dear, and we both know it. No, you are hiding something." Maude leaned forward slightly and darted out her hand to grip Cordelia's knee. "You must tell me."

I need to take some lessons on obfuscation and misdirection from Ruby, she thought. To Maude, she attempted to smile innocently. "No, Maude, it's nothing to worry about at all. But I must tell you that I am quite set upon my plan to write about regional foods. Did you see that Mrs James — that is not her real name, mark my words — has a column now in that weekly rag, the Illustrated this or that? They are hot for it in London, you know, this revival of the home-making arts."

"It never does to follow fashion," Maude sniffed. "And

now you have your house, you are hardly wanting for money." She cocked her head. "Or are you? Oh! Is that what you conceal? My dear, fret not. I can help. I know a man…"

"I need borrow nothing."

"Not to loan you money, silly girl. To marry you, of course. You must meet him. He has a jewel mine in South America."

"Lucky him. Thank you, but no. I am not for marrying again."

"Your mourning period is over."

Cordelia gritted her teeth briefly. It was an endless circular argument that she had had daily with her aunt.

Maude caught her expression of frustration, and this time she withdrew her attack. Instead, she returned to her first accusation.

"So," she said. "Ah! Now I have it. I know a very good doctor, and he can be here by tomorrow, I promise you."

"I am not ill. I am not in debt. There is nothing," Cordelia insisted.

"Oh, my dear—"

Cordelia looked up as footsteps approached. It was Ruby, a welcome sight. Her maid stopped just inside the door, and bobbed a reluctant curtsey towards Maude.

"My lady. There is a matter you might come to attend

to."

Cordelia rose but as she took her leave of Maude, her aunt said, "Let me give some advice, while we are talking like this. You allow your maid to be altogether too free in her manner. It will only come to ill, if you let her speak to you like this."

She meant, if Cordelia let Ruby speak first, unprompted. Cordelia inclined her head, mostly to hide her expression of stubborn refusal, and followed Ruby out of the room.

"I am too free, am I?" Ruby said as she led the way up the narrow stairs.

"Apparently so. I had always thought as much."

"I am so very sorry, my lady."

"You are a sarcastic minx who ought to be thrashed."

"Thank you, but there is a sad lack of strappingly handsome footmen around here to do the thrashing. You know I would bend most willingly to such discipline."

"Stop that at once!" Cordelia said, biting back her smile. "Now, what is this matter?"

Ruby stopped in the corridor outside their room, and lowered her voice. She pointed ahead to where there was an even tighter set of stairs than the flight they had just ascended. It led to the attic rooms.

"That Iris, the seamstress, is up there, in the room she

was sharing with Lizzie. She's in a state. I went up to see how she was doing. To be honest, I don't like her, but it didn't seem right that she be up there alone, in that room, now, like that, if you see."

"I do see."

"So she's crying, which I understand, and throwing her things into her trunk, and saying she means to leave."

"That is her right. Her work is to travel."

Ruby nodded. "But you might need to talk to her before she goes, my lady."

"Of course." Cordelia headed for the stairs. Iris would know many things — why Lizzie might have been at the Ally Cross, for a start.

Cordelia went up the stairs and peeked in past the open door. Iris had her back turned and was standing quite still, her head bent. Cordelia knocked gently, and the tall, willowy seamstress jumped and whirled around.

When she saw Cordelia, she bobbed a low curtsey and coloured a deep red immediately.

"Stand up; thank you, but do stand up," Cordelia said, coming into the room fully.

It was a long attic room with a sloping ceiling that made it feel poky and tight. There was a narrow bed either side of the door, and each bed had a dressing table the far side of it. The bed on the right was scattered with personal effects and clothing, and at the foot of it was a trunk.

"Iris, how do you fare?" Cordelia asked. She hadn't spoken more than two words to the young woman since her arrival; Iris had stayed well out of her way.

Iris had a narrow face with enormous eyes that were ringed by long, dark lashes. The hair on her head was ashy blonde, and altogether she had a fey look to her. She was dressed in sober but well-made clothes, as befitted her station as a dressmaker, and she was clutching a book from which a piece of paper was poking.

"My lady, I, I simply can't stay, it's all too awful," she said, keeping her eyes lowered.

"Indeed, it looks as if you are packing to leave."

Iris's narrow shoulders shrugged. "I can't stay here," she whispered.

"Of course." Lizzie McNab might not have been killed in the room but it bore her memory still; her own travelling chest was at the bottom of her bed, closed, and her things littered her dressing table. Cordelia noticed that the book Iris was clutching was the Bible, a battered and well-loved copy. "Where do you intend to go?"

"I — don't know." Iris sat down with a thump on her bed, and sighed.

Cordelia said, "Well, I am sure that there is no hurry, and I shall talk to Maude about finding you a different room to sleep in." Kate had been moved into a small room downstairs, a little offshoot near to the cook's room. *Surely somewhere similar could be found to Iris in a house of this size*, she thought.

Iris looked confused. "To sleep in?" she repeated.

"Yes, because—" Cordelia stopped. "Are you not bothered by sleeping here?"

"No, that's not it at all. I have no fear on that account. She has gone to a better place, one that I long to be, but it will be at our Saviour's direction, will it not? My destiny is not yet played out here. Oh — I am sorry, my lady, I prattle on." She bowed her head and her face was hidden by her uncurling hair.

Cordelia raised her eyebrows. *Well, what a girl indeed.* "Still," she went on, "you must not dash off with no aim and no place to go. Maude will let you stay on. I shall see to that."

"I will go tonight," Iris whispered. She stood up in a rush and returned to her packing, her elbows thrown out defiantly as she moved in that jerky movement all women did when they were trying to keep busy rather than cry.

"Have you family to go to?"

"No. No one."

Dead? Or simply estranged? Cordelia watched Iris fold a long summer gown carefully. "Iris, you seem to be a level-headed girl generally." *Apart from this matter of leaving so rashly.* "What of Lizzie? Can you tell me why she was at the Ally Cross yesterday?"

"Oh, my lady, it is not my place to talk of her. She and I, we were of different stations in life, were we not? I tried not to irritate her with my chit-chat."

"You had been sharing a room here for a few weeks."

"Indeed, my lady, and I sought to keep myself to myself and not to bother her. She did not appreciate the fact that I was moved into this room that had previously been hers. But … Miss Stanbury insisted I was not to be alone. We are not well trusted, you know…"

Cordelia sighed. "I am sorry for my aunt's presumptions. Now, let us be frank. Lizzie was meeting a man up there at the cross, was she not?" It was a landmark, well known, but out of the way; ideal for assignations.

Iris pushed the clothing down in her trunk, hard, and didn't look up. "Maybe she was, but I don't recall as she had any real sweetheart here. She perhaps cast her eye at one man or another. But I cannot speak of it. As I say, I do not really know. I am sorry, my lady."

Of course you'd know, Cordelia thought crossly, wanting to slap the simpering young woman. *You must know something.* But there was nothing more to be gained. She thanked her and went back down to her room to speak to Ruby. Perhaps her own maid would have more luck prising the right information out of Iris.

Ruby already knew more than Cordelia. She sat smugly in the armchair by the fire, mending some stockings. Her sewing was unwilling, but neat and relatively swift. She was glad of the interruption, though, and bundled it all back into the basket at her feet.

"Oh, yes, she definitely had a lover," Ruby said eagerly. "I would wager any amount that they were meeting up there; she would know that Maude would be at the church and so Lizzie was free to go."

"Tell me everything you know."

Ruby grimaced. "Unfortunately, that's all I do know. She had a man, and his name was Percy."

"Percy who? And just one man?"

"I know nothing more."

Cordelia paced in frustration. "But if you knew, and you have been here a few days, then Iris would have known this also. She should have told me."

"Iris is a funny old stick who seems to scuttle along apologising for her very existence," Ruby said. "She barely speaks. Which is exactly how your aunt likes it."

"This is ridiculous. We know she had a lover; that is the first place the police need to now look."

"There are no police," Ruby said. "That constable, and

that's it. No one wants to know."

"I want to know. I am going to—"

There was a knock at the door, and the general maid entered.

"Begging pardon, my lady," Kate said, keeping herself standing rigidly by the door. "There is a man here for you."

"Percy? Percy!" Cordelia said. "But how can that be?"

Kate shook her head. "He's in the kitchens, my lady. He is all dressed in black and has a limp and something of a … of a temper, my lady. Cook is crying in her room."

"Oh my goodness." Cordelia's eyes met Ruby's.

"Geoffrey."

CHAPTER FIVE

It was an awkward reunion.

"I have brought urgent news from Clarfields," he said, his flat voice lacking any urgency. He had risen to his feet when Cordelia entered the kitchen, but that was as far as his obsequiousness went. He held a hunk of bread in his wide hands, and he leaned back against the wooden table, one leg cocked and all his weight resting almost casually on his other leg. He had shed his outdoor jacket and hat, but was still swathed in many layers of dark clothing, which only served to emphasise his bulk.

His craggy, lined face had not been shaved for some days.

"How did you get here?" she demanded of her coachman.

"I rode, my lady. It was about as comfortable as you might expect."

"So what is this news that had you ride up from Surrey so hastily?" He must have been riding for days, she knew. Sending a letter by mail coach, or riding on the railways would have been quicker.

"Mrs Unsworth is drunk, mostly. I suppose that will not surprise you, though. Your butler has some idea to re-order the wine cellar and I would not trust him to do that without your supervision. There has been post for you, from London. I thought you would want to see it. Also, the staff want to put a large German tree in the hallway."

"They want to do what?"

"A tree, my lady. Since our good Queen adopted the fashion from her husband, it is all the rage. So they tell me."

Cordelia remembered the illustration that had appeared in the press a few years ago. She shook her head wryly. "What nonsense. But Geoffrey, now tell me the truth. Why are you *really* here?"

The coachman shrugged sullenly, and reached to his side to carve off an uneven hunk of cheese. "You needed to know these things. Also, it is likely time for you to come home, now Advent is begun. The roads are tricky at the moment, in this cold weather, and I do not think that Stanley has the skills to drive your carriage."

"Of course he does. He is a good boy with much promise." *Especially out from under your oppressive dominion.*

"And anyway, I had instructed you to remain at rest. *At rest,* Geoffrey. Your leg will not heal if you charge about on horses. And you know that I am only to stay here a fortnight." She quashed her memory of the recent events. Two weeks only, she told herself.

But Geoffrey always had been a force answerable only to himself. He had been her late husband's man, first, and his companion on her husband's escapades. When Cordelia had first arrived at Clarfields, he had treated her with silent contempt.

Until he had begun to witness the cruelty of Lord Cornbrook. Geoffrey's allegiances had changed, in an instant, and that switch had altered everything.

Couldn't he see that *that* was why she had insisted that he stay behind at Clarfields, and take some much-deserved rest? He had argued back, when she'd told him, and they had shared some strong words. She did not appreciate having her authority challenged so blatantly.

And now he was here, using their joint past as a justification for ignoring her orders.

She glared at him.

"My leg is perfectly well," he said eventually.

"And the doctor will attest to that, will he?"

He grunted. "There was no need for me to be bothering your expensive doctor man. I am healed, my lady, and there it is. Now, a fresh cup of tea?" He looked around the small kitchen hopefully. There was no sign of cook. Ruby tossed her head and flounced away immediately. Cordelia beckoned Kate forward.

"Would you?"

Kate looked quite terrified. She pressed herself against the far cupboards to sidle her way around to the range.

"Be nice to her," Cordelia said. "I shall go and advise my aunt of your unexpected arrival."

* * *

The local and national newspapers picked up the story of the "lovelorn girl found brutally murdered." Maude might have hoped that it was only a small matter which would soon blow over, but once one paper got wind of it, they all wanted to outdo one another in their wild speculation and rumour. Every "Herald" and "Gazette" and "News" produced illustrated treatises on the events, labelled as "fact" while they were actually closer to Penny Dreadfuls in their tone and content. But they sold well. After all, murders were very rare, and the general public clamoured for sensational happenings.

Or, "the seething mass of the lower sorts seek to sink lower and lower in their pursuit of degradation and filth," as Maude put it, on Saturday at lunch.

Cordelia tried to fold the regional Herald into a more

manageable reading shape. "They are saying today that it was her lover, this Percy Slatters, and that he is an officer in the Hussars!" The name matched what Ruby had heard.

"There you have it, then," Maude said sourly. "They must arrest him and hang him. Enough with the press and the rags, Cordelia. Put it aside. Must we have this at every meal?"

"Of course. Do forgive me." She folded it away. She was still clinging on, tentatively, to Maude's good side, even though her aunt had grumbled somewhat at Geoffrey's extra mouth to feed.

Cordelia had gleaned other titbits of information from the newspapers, but she had no idea how accurate they all were. The general consensus was that the local official, William Gold, was looking into it, and that the body was still laid out in a local inn, being viewed and considered. It was suggested by one paper that for a small sum, the curious onlooker might gain admittance. Cordelia believed it, and shuddered.

Most of the papers were pegging it as a crime of passion. Cordelia wondered about the poor family who had come to beg for work for their boy; Lizzie had treated them with contempt. It did not seem like enough of a motive, however, and Cordelia resolved to keep that to herself. Had Maude mentioned it to Gold? No doubt he'd seize upon the information.

But the manner of death had not yet been fully agreed upon. William Gold had sent for an eminent doctor from Leeds, and they were awaiting the esteemed man's arrival. There had been three local doctors who had all proclaimed something different, and according to one paper, there had been a scene of fisticuffs and abuse between the learned gentlemen.

One said she had been poisoned with opium, but another said that the traces were not of a fatal dose, and that she had been suffocated. The third pooh-poohed it all and declared that she had simply been overwrought with love or some strong emotion, and had expired in her lover's arms, and that it was not his fault at all for clearly being so dashing and handsome, and that he ought to confess all and that he would be quite safe, because men could not help their effect on women.

Ruby had nearly laughed herself sick when Cordelia told her that, after lunch, when they were dressing to go out for a walk.

"Now, my lady," she said as her chortles subsided, "is this a normal walk or are we playing at constables?"

"Well, as the rain has stopped, I think we need to go and talk to people," Cordelia said. "I have been no further than the church. There is a whole thriving town out there for us to explore! And I mean to track down this Percy Slatters."

"If he is with the Hussars, won't he be garrisoned in somewhere larger, like York?" Ruby said.

"I think Stoneyford is large enough to have the soldiers there. Anyway, first we need to talk to others. I will track down his reputation."

"You'll end up with a preformed opinion of the man," Ruby said. She pulled on her outdoor gloves and wrapped a thick, old, but serviceable cloak around her shoulders. "I would say that you ought to meet him before you listen to gossip."

"Hush now."

"I'm right, aren't I?"

She was. Cordelia harrumphed her way to the door. "I am sure I can rise above being tainted by common slander."

"It's the uncommon sort I'm interested in," Ruby muttered as she followed her mistress out into the cold, damp air.

* * *

It was a mile to the town of Stoneyford. The track that led away from Four Trees was rough and rocky until they reached the church. From there, it was a little better maintained. They had passed that way in the pouring rain when they had arrived, and Cordelia had not taken much note of her surroundings.

"You know, the views are remarkably fine, I would imagine, in the summer," Cordelia said as they paused for breath at the top of a small rise. The church lay behind them now. The track was wider here, though still rocky, and they had to pick their way through mud and pools of standing water. Cordelia took a few steps up the scrubby bank and looked out over the wide grey moors. "Which way to the Ally Cross?"

Ruby scrambled up to join her. She pointed up. "Follow that line to the left, that grey wall, and then you will see a path part from it and head in a curve to the right. That's the pack horse route. And you can just make out the smudge that is the cross on the horizon."

"I see."

"Let us not go there today."

The sky was gloomy and the clouds hung low. The distant hills were shades of grey-green, growing fainter as they receded, and the very air felt wet. Sheep straggled across the sparse fields. There were squat buildings every few miles, but many of them looked abandoned. Only a handful had smoke rising from the chimneys.

Cordelia nodded. "I think we shall leave it for another day. I am not certain of what I would learn there, anyway. I shall leave the picking around for evidence to the constable and Mr Gold and the doctors. I am interested in the people connected to all of this."

Together they slithered back to the track. They walked on until they saw a high wall ahead of them. "Though the hills be wild and romantic, I do prefer views of civilisation," Ruby said. "What lies that way?"

They approached the wall which met the road ahead of them and turned at a right angle to follow their path. Eventually they came to a large set of gates and through the ornate ironwork they could see a fine and newly-built house.

The brass plate screwed to the stone pillars declared it to be Stoney Mill House.

"Ah!" Cordelia said. "This is Simeon's place. We are to have a soiree here soon."

Ruby wrapped her gloved hands around the cold ironwork of the gate. "How sad. It looks like a lovely place. But he lives there alone now, doesn't he?"

"He does, since his wife died and all his sons went off to make their own ways."

"No daughters to stay and look after him?"

"None. But he has his mill to look after."

"You'd think that his sister-in-law would move in with him to help keep house."

Cordelia laughed. "Maude? She has lived at Four Trees her whole life and there would be no prising her out of there. It was her mill — her family's mill — before Simeon married into the family. She'll not leave there, and he had this place built for his wife so he won't leave here."

"Why are the gates locked?" Ruby said suddenly, stepping back.

"I don't know. Privacy? Habit?"

"He's afraid of something."

"Maybe the fact that there is a murderer roaming these hills. The papers are full of it."

"They are full of something, indeed," Cordelia muttered. "Much like a midden is."

They continued on their walk towards the town. As they crested the next hill, they saw that Stoneyford itself was a large and bustling place. Down in the valley they could see a rash of grey terraced housing, all packed together for warmth. A river ran through the middle, and the houses butted right up against it. The track was now roughly cobbled.

Between them and the town was a large, dark mill building.

And between them and the mill was a mob.

"Goodness," Cordelia said, feeling slightly intimidated. "Is it their lunch break, do you suppose?"

Ruby eyed the mass of brown-clad men and women who were milling about on the road about three hundred yards ahead of them, down in a dip. "Not unless they eat fresh air, though they look poor enough that I'd believe it."

"There must be a hundred or so."

"More," said Ruby. "Count ten and see how large a group that is compared to the whole. I'd say one hundred and fifty. Children, too."

There were, indeed, smaller figures creeping around the legs of the adults.

"What is their aim, their purpose?" Cordelia said. "Has there been a hue and cry raised?"

"Perhaps, but no one looks like they know what they are doing. There are no soldiers or constables or any officials. They are just there, waiting."

"So what do we do?"

"We go and find out." Ruby glanced up at her mistress. "Don't worry. I'll protect you."

"From a score of hungry workers?"

"Hm. Yes. Perhaps it is better if you wait here, then, my lady. I shall go and investigate." Ruby strode down the path to the nearest knot of women.

Cordelia watched anxiously as Ruby spoke with the crowd. There was much angry arm waving, and one person turned away with a dismissive look on their face. But Ruby soon returned, unharmed, beckoning Cordelia to come and meet her.

"The factory is closed today," Ruby explained. "It's on short time for lack of work."

"Oh."

"So these people have all been turned off their shift early, and are angry, because they want the work. It is winter, and times are hard; they need the money."

"But if there is no work, what can Simeon do?"

Ruby sighed. "Mr Welsh has a large, fine house and food and money and carriages and clothes and all the wealth of a gentleman. And he is a good man, so they all say. These people work hard for him and they are pleased to do so. But, my lady, it is a contract between him and the townsfolk. They work — and he gives them work. They feel cheated, somehow."

"They think he's let them down?"

"Exactly so."

"But even if he were to unlock his gates and let them all swarm over his house, in a week when all his food is gone, what then?"

"A week hence is impossible to think of when your belly's empty this moment, my lady, and your children cry for lack of porridge."

"If I go down there, they will attack me."

Ruby shook her head. "No, they won't. As I say, it is between Mr Welsh and them; not you. These are honourable folk."

Cordelia was gripped by doubt. While she demurred and hesitated, the crowd's attention suddenly sharpened. Heads turned in one direction. The people began to move to one side, and pack together more closely.

And a dark-haired figure, bare-headed, climbed onto the back of a cart, rising up above the crowd with his fist in the air.

"It is that man again," Ruby said.

Her maid seemed to feel the same compulsion to draw near that the crowd was also feeling. And Cordelia, too, felt herself dragged towards him. She and Ruby pressed in close with the others, now, and no one looked their way. All attention was on the man who was waiting, silently, to address the crowd.

"Who is he?" Cordelia said to the man next to her. He was dressed in clean but patched working clothes, and he looked startled to be addressed by her. But he answered, in his thick accent.

"That, ma'am, is Mr John Kitt. He speaks here from time to time. Lately come again from Manchester, I hear."

"And what does he speak of?"

The man narrowed his eyes and looked at her as if she were trying to trick him. "Ma'am, he is one of the petitioners for free men."

"I do not follow," Cordelia said.

Ruby spoke up. "He's a Chartist, my lady."

"Of course." She had heard the word muttered outside the church, too.

Cordelia realised that she was the only person still speaking. The crowd was silent, their faces turned expectantly to the man on the cart. Though he stood still, his body seemed to be filled with a tightly-coiled dynamism. *Maybe it was the tautness in his jaw, or the way his shoulders were thrown back,* Cordelia thought. He looked like he could snatch up a stick and parry with it as if it were a sword.

The silence lengthened. He didn't speak until people were actually holding their breaths, waiting for his words.

He began quietly, so that people had to strain to hear him. "Once again, my friends, my countrymen, you are here, lost and alone in your own town. Your town! Yours! Yet you are powerless. You think you should be within the walls of that factory, and you yearn to put yourselves back into the yoke of the master."

Some nodded, and one man cried out, "Yes! We need work!"

"No!" John Kitt roared, his shout splitting the air. The hairs rose on the back of Cordelia's neck. "You need *freedom!* You seek subservience to an unfeeling system that will give you nothing! It will take all, and leave you drained and dry and dead. The old order is broken, I tell you!"

"But we need to work," the man said stubbornly, though more quietly.

"When you are there in that mill, you are not a working man. You're a dog, a donkey, nothing more than a fleshy body that will be used and then cast aside. You have no power, no say, yet it is only by the sweat of your brow that this factory works at all! You have the power and you give it up, to them. And you let them keep it."

John Kitt paused and threw back his head. He took his time gazing around the crowd, letting his eyes rest on each person, or so it felt.

A murmuring rose, then fell. Into the silence, he spoke again. "And how do you think they keep the power for themselves?"

"They have the money. They always have," muttered a woman to one side, but no one spoke up directly. Kitt waited for a moment before continuing.

"They make the laws! They are the ones in parliament, setting the taxes and favouring themselves, their families, their businesses. *We* need to have a say in the laws that affect us!"

"Who cares about laws?" someone was bold enough to shout.

"Who cares?" John Kitt shouted in the direction of the

challenger. "These laws are corrupt. These laws will do nothing for us. A few days ago, a girl was killed here and what will they do? Nothing. It's a tale to sell some newspapers but that is all. Will you take that? Do you accept that? They can kill us and nothing happens! Peterloo! Remember the massacre."

Cordelia shivered. She had not been born at the time of the tragic events in Manchester, but it was still living memory to many of the older people in the crowd. The cavalry had charged an assembly of tens of thousands of people agitating for parliamentary reform, and had hacked indiscriminately at the unarmed protestors. Hundreds were injured, and fifteen lost their lives.

And nothing had changed. Two petitions had been given to parliament by the Chartists so far, pressing for change, and still the world turned as it had always done.

Now he was shouting about the failure of those petitions, and how if peaceful democratic means did not work, then the people had to turn to other methods.

"My lady, he is calling for violence," Ruby said in Cordelia's ear. She pulled urgently at Cordelia's arm. "The mood may turn at any minute. We should go."

"I would not want to be caught between this mob and Simeon's mill or house."

"Indeed. Come away."

Cordelia let herself be drawn from the crowd. They stepped back slowly, and were soon at the edge. People were surging forward, and there were more cries of support than of protest at John Kitt's words.

Cordelia turned to look back over the gathering. "They hang upon his every word now."

"They do. This is dangerous."

"Yet I feel some sympathy for their plight."

"Indeed," Ruby said neutrally.

They walked briskly, looking back from time to time, in fear of seeing the mob amassing behind them. Their way home was clear, however, and soon they were back in the grounds of Four Trees.

Cordelia stopped on the gravelled area in front of the house, and looked up. "We had a wasted journey," she said sadly. "But I am determined no more time should be lost. I will return to the town by carriage, tomorrow, and speak to whom I may, and perhaps venture on to the next nearest town too, and seek out the magistrate, Mr Gold, if I can, if he is not at Stoneyford."

Instead of going inside the house, she went around the side, to the stables. Stanley was in the tack room, huddled by an oil lamp though it gave precious little warmth. He was applying saddle soap to a bridle. The rich smell always pleased Cordelia and she breathed in deeply.

"My lady," he said, jumping up.

"Ah, Stanley," she said, waving him back to his task. "I will need you to drive me to town tomorrow. Have the carriage ready after breakfast."

"But church—"

"Dash it. Of course, you will want to go. I understand. Where is Geoffrey? Since he claims he is fully fit, he may as well be useful."

Stanley flushed red and looked down. His stammer worsened as he said, "I do not know, my lady."

"If you don't know, why do you react so?" Cordelia said.

"I — he — went to the town, Stoneyford."

"When?"

"Two hours ago."

He had left before they had, and so that was why he had not been spotted. "What did he do there? Seeking the alehouse, was he?"

"No, my lady, he said he went to see a man called Kitt."

"Do you know who that man is?"

"No, my lady."

"Do you remember that man who was speaking outside the church last week? That was he; John Kitt."

Even Stanley's ears were bright red now. He flicked his gaze upwards, briefly looking at Cordelia's face. That was how she knew he was seriously concerned. He said, painfully slowly, "My lady, I fear there might be something amiss. Geoffrey has secrets, my lady, and he talks in a strange way about…"

"About what?"

"Revolution."

CHAPTER SIX

"This book of yours," Maude said at Sunday breakfast. "How goes it?"

"I thought that *you* thought it was all nonsense."

Maude glared briefly at Cordelia. She folded her cloth napkin and waved at Kate, who darted forward to retrieve her plate. As she took the crockery, her hand shook, and Maude said, "Stop!"

Kate froze.

"You should move more quietly. I should not hear the cutlery clatter on the plate."

"No, ma'am. Sorry, ma'am."

"Go."

Kate dashed away.

"I still think it is nonsense," Maude continued. "But if you decide to pursue nonsense then you must do so wholeheartedly. I thought you would be interviewing people, doing research, making notes, that sort of thing. A wishy-washy woman is worse than a misguided one."

"I am pursuing it," Cordelia said. "In fact, I am heading into town today to begin."

"Who are you meeting?"

Ah, so that was why Maude was interested. She just wants to keep a close eye on my doings. "I thought I might ... um. I thought I might look in the ..." Cordelia stopped. She wanted to see the sort of street food that was sold, and send Ruby into eating houses.

She wondered what Maude would say to all that.

"You should go to York," Maude said. "Or Harrogate. That's closer, and there are respectable people there. But to my mind, good food is good food, wherever you are."

"Indeed. But the food of the common person varies so much from place to place. Here, they don't talk so much of bread. It's oats, and porridge."

Maude shrugged. "Give us this day our daily bread," she intoned. "And they ought to be grateful for it. You are coming to church, are you not? You had best hurry with your breakfast."

In the end, Cordelia, Maude and Ruby rode in the carriage to church. As it was not raining, Stanley took Maude back to Four Trees after another unintelligible sermon. Ruby and Cordelia walked on into town, much to

Maude's muttered disgust.

"We will find and speak to Percy Slatters," Cordelia said. "And as many people as we can who know of him. I also want to speak to the magistrate if he's here, and all who knew Lizzie."

The town was quieter than the previous day. They passed the area where John Kitt had been speaking from his cart, and the ground was churned up. There were scraps of clothing in amongst the rocks and mud.

"Was there an altercation here, do you think?" Cordelia said to Ruby, pointing at some broken fence that lay between an open area and someone's garden.

"Maybe." Ruby hailed a passing woman, who was carrying a baby in a rough fabric sling nestled under her shawl. "What happened here yesterday?"

The young woman had few teeth in her thin-lipped face. "I dunno. They was carrying-on and then the soldiers came."

"Was anyone hurt?"

The woman shrugged and the movement set the baby off crying. "Mayhap a few split skulls, I dunno. Stay out of it, that's what I say."

"Thank you."

The woman hesitated until she saw she was to receive no coin for her information. She set her mouth in a grim line and scuttled away.

"We are definitely going to find the garrison," Cordelia said.

Ruby scurried to keep up. "Right, my lady, and what then? You march into the barracks, do you?"

"Yes, I do."

"Protected by…"

"My status," Cordelia said. "And I have seen sparring matches. I am sure I could land a hefty blow. I read a book on the boxing arts, you know, once."

"Really?" There was a sceptical tone in Ruby's voice that immediately had Cordelia's hackles up. She determined, then, to somehow get herself into a fight so that she could prove herself to her maid. She flexed her right hand within its fine fur-lined winter glove.

They progressed along a cobbled street. There were shops along here, now, and many of them were still open though they would soon be closing for their Sunday half-day. The rest of the week, they would be open until ten in the evening, or later; otherwise, the working folk would have no chance to buy anything after their long shifts ended at the mill. The shops were small, with dark windows and even more shadowy interiors, and Cordelia wasn't exactly sure what some of them were even selling.

They came to a more respectable-looking milliners',

and Cordelia sent Ruby in to ask for directions to the garrison. Ruby came out after only a minute, looking rather angry.

"He assumed I was seeking the soldiers to perform certain female services for them," she said sniffily, leading Cordelia away with haste. "And then he offered to test out my services."

"Oh dear," Cordelia said. "I expect you assured him that the footmen of southern England had already performed that duty thoroughly?"

"My lady!"

Cordelia giggled to herself as they turned a corner, and were suddenly faced with an impressive-looking building of double height, with rows of small, square windows, and a man with a scarlet pelisse over his shoulder at the gatehouse.

And very smart he would have been, too, if he had not been asleep on his stool, his body wedged upright between a stone pillar and the wall.

Cordelia kicked him awake.

He lurched forward and tried to grab his ankle, his sword and his stool, all at the same time. His shako fell off his head and tumbled along the street.

He swore, looked up, saw he was in the presence of a lady, and threw himself after his errant hat.

"My lady, ma'am, madam, I am sorry," he gabbled, shoving the dented shako back on his head, and attempting a poor salute. His eyes slid sideways. "I wasn't asleep," he added in a lowered voice. "It was an … I'm on undercover … my duty is unusual … I'm a decoy," he announced. "That is it, entirely."

"Gosh," Cordelia said, doing her best effort at a girlie simper. "What a fantastic role you were playing. I was utterly convinced. I can see why our British Army is such a feared fighting force across the globe!"

Ruby tutted.

The not-quite-watchman looked from one to the other, and confusion began to cross his reddened face. "Ma'am, is there anything I can help you with? We don't receive many ladies here."

"Oh, I hear that you do," Cordelia said, trying to flutter her eyelashes. "Why, we have been hearing all over town that *ladies* are always welcome here. Day or *night*."

The soldier looked absolutely horrified as he sought for a way to explain the more sordid ways of the world to an apparently fine and innocent lady and her maid. "I — that is — perhaps people have been confused and spoke of — there is — I shall fetch my commanding officer!" he finished in a rush. "Please, do wait here."

He hurled himself through the arch and into a

courtyard beyond.

Cordelia slid a sideways glance at Ruby, who was caught halfway between embarrassment and admiration. Cordelia grinned briefly before composing her expression back to a respectable half-smile. "Come, Ruby. Let us explore."

"Perhaps we ought to wait…"

"I am a lady. I do not wait." Cordelia sashayed into the courtyard.

Everything was very still and quiet. She wasn't sure what she was expecting, but she had hoped for some glimpses of men on parade, or practising their firing drills, or something. She had seen soldiers when they had ridden past at spectacles, and of course she had seen countless paintings in galleries and collections.

The reality seemed to be one of slumber, and if the watchman was anything to go on, ineptitude.

She gazed around at the double-height buildings on all four sides. Passageways led out from the back of the square, presumably to stables and storerooms and the like.

"Now what?" Ruby asked, appearing at Cordelia's elbow. "Are you actually going to hammer on a door and burst into the sleeping quarters?"

Cordelia took one step towards the nearest door but she wasn't quite sure what she was going to do; luckily at that moment she was saved from her rash impulsivity by the stocky, squat figure of a man striding towards her from one of the far passageways.

"Madam!" he boomed in some alarm, and speeded up.

"Good day," she said. "Are you the commanding officer?"

"No, madam. I am afraid that Captain Slatters is called away presently. I am Sergeant Bloom. I fear there may have been a misunderstanding."

"I think not. It is Captain Slatters — Percy Slatters, yes? — that I was hoping to see."

The sergeant shook his head. "Then you are sadly disappointed. I do not know when he returns."

"I see. Tell me, my good man, about this place. You are all keen fighting men, are you?"

The sergeant was still shaking his head, making the horsehair plume on his shako waft in the air. *Sergeant-Says-No*, she thought. "We're part-time," he explained. "This is just a troop of the Yorkshire Hussars Yeomanry. These men are farmers and tradesmen, volunteers, made ready for the possible riots as we did three years back at Cleckheaton, putting down the Luddites."

"I see. Well, you do look very smart and I am sure we shall all rest easier in our beds, knowing you are ready to quell any uprising. Speaking of which, what transpired yesterday?"

The plume quivered and waved left to right. "Ma'am, you need have no fear. Some low sorts sought to cause trouble but they were soon dispersed."

"Any injuries?"

"All my men are hale and hearty."

"I mean, among the others. The public."

The head-shaking threatened to dislodge his hat. "I have no idea. They brought it upon themselves."

Cordelia had lost her smile by this point. She forced herself to look calm and benign. "Tell me about your officer, then, this Captain Slatters. What manner of man is he?"

"I — do not know what to say, ma'am. He is our commander. He is of the 13th Light Dragoons and sent to oversee us, ma'am. That is all I can really say."

"He is a good officer?"

"He is like any other."

She realised she was at an impasse with him. She would have been better trying to quiz the guard on duty at the gate, she thought. She gave up, bid him good day, and retreated out onto the street.

As soon as they were out of earshot, Ruby spoke. She said, simply, "No."

"What do you mean?" Cordelia said.

"You are about to ask me to go back into the barracks, possibly under the cover of darkness, and to use my feminine talents to talk to, or about, Percy Slatters. I don't think you appreciate what that would involve."

"I am shocked and appalled." Cordelia clicked her tongue as she pretended to think about the idea. It had, of course, been the first thing she'd considered. "However, now you mention it … you are such a bright girl to come up with these ideas, you know."

"And if Percy, as the lover of Lizzie, did murder her …?"

"I think we could acquire a pistol for you. A small sort, easily hidden in your skirts."

"My lady, you do not pay me enough for this."

"Perhaps not." Cordelia sighed. "Well, then. We have more to discover. Let us seek out the magistrate!"

"Oh, how wonderful," Ruby muttered as she trailed behind.

* * *

Cordelia headed back to the main street of the town, which was wide and pleasant. Clearly, a row of buildings had been knocked down in some civic improvement exercise, because all the other roads were narrow and poky. Halfway down the high street was a comfortable and respectable-looking coaching inn.

"If Mr Gold is here, then this is where we'll find him lodging," Cordelia said. "If he is not, then tomorrow I propose a trip to Harrogate. And I have always had a fancy to visit the Royal Pump Room and take the waters."

"Certainly they are said to have invigorating effects," Ruby said. "I shouldn't think you have need of them at all."

"How rude of you," Cordelia said without malice. They ascended the steps and were met in the hallway of the inn by a frilly-capped maid, who bobbed at them. They could see half-glazed doors leading off in all directions, with gilt lettering announcing the 'Saloon Bar' for the middle classes, and the 'Public Bar' for the lower sorts.

"Would you like a snug? A booth or private room, madam?" the maid asked, well-trained in assessing a customer's potential worth.

"Actually, we are seeking the Justice of the Peace," Cordelia said.

"Mr Gold?" The maid's eyebrows flickered but that was all the emotion that registered on her professional face. "Well, certainly he lodges here, but he may not be available. Let me show you to a room, and bring you drinks while you wait. I shall make enquiries. Follow me."

Cordelia knew she was being shunted into purchasing drinks that she didn't really want, but she had no choice. She and Ruby were installed in a small, comfortable sitting room that had every inch of its red-papered walls covered with prints and paintings of hunting scenes. The horses had spindly legs that looked unlikely to support their oddly square bodies, and all the men were gallant and slender.

The maid brought drinks but no word of William Gold. Cordelia had ordered hot cocoa for them both, with a dash of brandy added, to help keep the cold at bay. They sipped at them while they waited.

Cordelia was starting to suspect they were going to be kept until they had ordered three more rounds of drinks and a full meal to stave off starvation, when at last the door opened, but it was not a fine magisterial figure that appeared there.

"Oho, Lady Cornbrook, and your bonny maid also!" rumbled the thoroughly unwelcome sight of the parish constable, David Kennett. He pulled the door closed behind him and stood there with his back to it, smiling as if he were faced with a feast of delicacies all for himself.

Cordelia's heart sank. She remained seated, and gripped her empty mug. It would possibly serve as a weapon, she thought, even if its main service would be one of surprise.

"Ah, Mr Kennett. We are waiting to see Mr Gold."

"He's out on business," Kennett said brusquely. He let his gaze linger on them for a moment before suddenly speaking at exhaustive length. "But as his authorised deputy in all matters as pertains to this area, and so forth, you may speak quite freely with me, and I shall decide what needs to be passed on to Mr Gold. He is an awfully busy man, you know. Well, you shan't know, I imagine. I speak not of knitting. As Justice of the Peace, he covers such a wide area, and is frightfully in demand, and so on."

"I see," Cordelia said. "And when will he be back?"

"As to that, I may not comment, you see, perhaps, or maybe you don't, aha, with his business and so forth, but he might be delayed and anyway, he did not give me a time to expect him."

"You do not know, in short."

"Exactly so, my lady, quite that, indeed."

Yes would suffice, she thought. *Well, when life gives you tripe, you make sausages.* "What news of the awful crime, Mr Kennett?" she asked.

He sucked in his breath and inflated his chest. "It is hardly fit for ladies to speak of, you know, with the murder and so forth, it is not decent."

"The newspapers are full of talk and I can hardly avoid it," she said. "But I imagine that someone as well-placed as you would have the true facts. I would trust the word of no other."

"You flatter me, my lady," he said. "But it is true, indeed, that I am in a position of great privilege…"

He was going to be privileged to be beaten about the head with an empty mug of cocoa if he does not get to the point, she thought as he rambled on. Eventually he said, "…and so the eminent doctor has concluded that she was poisoned, without a doubt."

"Goodness. With opium?"

"Indeed, with that much-misused medicine, the poor girl, yet of course, to be out on the moors as she was, one must question her morals, must one not? For women to be out without protection…" He looked at them both meaningfully. "Of course, you are both safe here, under *my* protection." He licked his lips.

But there was noise coming up from the bar below, and they could hear footsteps from time to time passing the door. She realised that though he wanted to push his luck, they were actually rather more safe here than when he had come visiting the isolated manor of Four Trees.

"How comforting," she murmured. "So, Mr Kennett, has your superior knowledge and skills revealed any hint of who might have done this awful deed?"

"As to that, I cannot rightly say, with any certainty, yet, although, it may be supposed, of course, that the popular gossip is very wrong."

"The popular gossip? Oh, I do not follow that; do explain, if you can."

"Well, madam, of course, I should not wish to taint your ears with my allusions to profane deeds and so forth but it is said that the poor girl must have been killed by a lover. And I can tell you that it is self-evident that popular gossip is incorrect!"

Is it drink that makes him ramble on so? When Cordelia had met the man the first time, he had smelled strongly of alcohol and had lurched from side to side, flailing to find a secure footing on an apparently flat piece of ground. The inn was a confusion of smells, however, and she was not sure if he was under the influence at the moment. She imagined that his face was always red, and his hands always shook. "Can you elaborate?" she asked. "Concisely?"

Eventually he staggered to the conclusion. "…poisoning being a woman's crime, and so on."

"Indeed." And indeed it was, she thought. But then, might not a clever man use it to appear as if a woman had done it? She didn't voice that thought. It would only spark a long ramble from Kennett and it would probably include his horror that any man would be so dishonourable.

"Thank you so much for coming to see us," she said.

He didn't take the obvious hint that it was now time for him to leave. He oozed half a step forward, which in the small room was quite far enough. "It was entirely my pleasure." He lowered his voice and spoke breathily, directing it straight at Cordelia. "Now, madam, if I might be so bold as to offer my assistance and so forth in returning you to the safety of your aunt's house, then I shall call for your coach and have it brought around."

"Thank you, but we are not ready to leave."

"Are you sure?" He simpered. "Tell me, then, when you intend to go and I shall—"

She cut him off, fed up now with his presence. "Thank you, but no. We are meeting friends and will be escorted home at a later hour. Good day," she added, firmly.

Reluctantly and by slow degrees, he exited.

"My lady, why did you say that?"

"He wanted to be in a coach with us, together … did you like that idea?"

Ruby shuddered. "Ah, no. And of course; you didn't want him to know that we would be walking home, unaccompanied."

"Exactly so. He would have fallen on us in an instant, if he thought he could."

"Did I not say so, before?"

"You did, Ruby. I am wise to listen to you. Tell me another thing. Was this a woman's crime?"

"If so," Ruby said, "what woman?"

Cordelia finally put her cold cup back on the tray. "Iris has not left Four Trees at all, has she? She has remained, after all."

"No. I think you persuaded her to see sense, my lady."

"Me? I wonder if that was the reason, indeed."

CHAPTER SEVEN

They walked back into Four Trees and straight into the middle of an argument.

Kate, the daily maid who had now been pressed into living in, was standing in Maude's private sitting room, holding her knobbly hands tightly together. Maude was seated, but she gripped the arms of her chair as if she was intending to launch herself upright.

"Tell her," Maude said, pointing at Kate as Cordelia came to a stop just within the door. "Tell this silly girl what's expected of her now."

Out of the corner of her eye, Cordelia saw Ruby melt away. Cordelia sighed and came into the room. "What is the problem, dear aunt?"

"This silly hussy won't have work. Think you might go to the mill, do you? I shall say not."

"I would rather work here than the mill, as always,

ma'am," Kate whispered. "But even a live-in has the right to a half-day off."

"Where does it say that?"

"In the Bible, begging pardon, ma'am. The day of rest. It is written."

Maude hissed. "Don't you be quoting scripture at me when I don't think you can read a single word. Wash your mouth out. It's a disgrace."

"I cannot be your live-in any longer," Kate continued. "I cannot work all day and every day. I have a right to keep the Sabbath."

"You have a *duty* to the mistress of this house! Me!"

Cordelia wished she still had the cocoa mug to hurl at her aunt's head. She said, "My dear Maude, the girl is quite right, you know. You cannot expect her to work endlessly."

This was the final straw for Maude, who rose unsteadily to her feet. She grabbed a cane that lay by the arm of the chair, and waved it in a shaky circle in front of her. "And who will be here to look after me, then, if you all go dilly-dallying away for a day!"

"Perhaps you ought to be advertising for a new companion," Cordelia said. "Or even consider a move into Stoney Mill House with your brother-in-law…"

"Ah! Someone speaks of me?"

Cordelia hadn't heard Simeon Welsh approach from

behind, and she half-jumped as he appeared a few feet away. She moved into the room to let him enter. He glanced around and took in the air of tension straight away.

It must have been a perennial argument with previous staff, because he seemed to grasp instantly what the matter was. He said, "Ah, Kate, what a surprise to see you still here *on your day off.* Why not run along now, and visit your family."

She dithered for a moment, then bobbed an uncertain curtsey and ran from the room.

Maude subsided back into her chair and did not have a welcoming expression on her face. Cordelia wanted to take her leave, but first she said to Simeon, "I missed you at the service this morning. Is everything all right with the mill?"

"You've heard, haven't you?" he said, as quick as ever. "There has been some unrest but the Yeomanry are here and available."

"They need to arrest that troublemaker, that John Kitt," Maude said from the depths of her armchair. "Hang him up and be done with it."

"Now, now, my dear," Simeon said. "We live under the rule of law."

"The law is made by us, for us," Maude said. "I don't see why such a rabble-rouser should be allowed to roam free. Do you know, he was here, hanging around! He dared to come onto my property. He gave his evil literature to poor Lizzie, trying to turn that maid's head. I saw him off. People like him need to be hanged."

This was an argument that Cordelia had no stomach for. She said, "Please do excuse me. I am just returned from a long walk, and need to rest. Dear aunt, shall I send for Iris to sit with you? I understand she has been persuaded to stay a little longer."

"Oh, that silent statue? She may as well leave for all I care, excepting that she needs to adjust my gown *again*. I ask for it to be lengthened and she adds a yard. I then tell her to take it up and it becomes positively indecent. No, you may leave her the well alone to get on with her duties."

Cordelia withdrew.

CHAPTER EIGHT

Maude ranted her way through dinner on Sunday night, and similarly through breakfast on Monday morning. Cordelia's head was full of fog and bitten-back retorts when she finally escaped back onto the road with Ruby. Once again, she had asked for Geoffrey to drive her to town. When she had gone down the steps to the courtyard, however, it was Stanley who jumped down from the driver's seat.

"Where is he?" she demanded.

Stanley stammered a denial that he knew anything at all, and Cordelia believed him. Anyway, she knew that Geoffrey thought the boy was too honest. The coachman was unlikely to impart any information to Stanley that he wanted to keep private.

"I mean to find this Percy Slatters," she told both Stanley and Ruby as they drew up in the centre of town. A waterer saw an opportunity for some money-making and dashed forward to see to the horses. "It might mean we trawl the countryside here about, if he is not at the barracks. Time is running out; although I will stay a little while longer, I simply *must* be back at Clarfields for Christmas."

"Should we split up?" Ruby asked.

"Yes. Stanley, you stay with the horse, but keep your ears open to all information. Ruby, you know where I want you to go."

"The barracks," she said, with a sigh. Cordelia had persuaded her during the carriage ride. "At least you're not suggesting I go there at night this time. Well, I suppose I might find some sort of diversion there."

"Make it a profitable one, if so," Cordelia instructed. "I shall go to the inn and make inquiries there, but this time I want to avoid that constable. And that zealous maid." Cordelia had dressed down, today, in the hope of seeming less intimidating; looking less exalted would increase her chances of getting into the saloon bar, at least.

Ruby strode off towards the garrison building, and Cordelia approached the inn, but waited until a well-dressed couple ascended the steps. She slipped in straight after them, and was through the saloon door before the maid had a chance to look up from her conversation with the couple.

It was a thriving place, with gleaming brass rails and many semi-private booths along the walls where people were being served whatever food they felt appropriate for the gap between breakfast and lunch. Cordelia was still out of place, but she hoped she looked more like a middle tradesman's wife made good than a lady who was slumming it.

Still, heads turned, although that might have been the general curiosity that townsfolk would have to strangers, especially in the dead of winter. She smiled around, and approached the bar. There was a woman there who seemed to be made of floury dumplings; her round white face was flaky and her eyes disappeared above ripe cheeks as she smiled in greeting.

Cordelia wasted no time. "Does the Captain of the Yeomanry, a certain Percy Slatters, ever come in here?" She was hoping that an officer would patronise the more salubrious drinking establishments. Otherwise, she would have to call on Geoffrey — if she could find the infuriating man — to trawl around some desperate dives in the town, the beerhouses and the like.

The plump woman nodded at a man who looked up as he heard his name mentioned. "There, madam, you see the man himself."

"Ah." Cordelia took a moment to survey him coolly.

He was a long, lean man with a flourishing sandy moustache and a wide grin showing even, white teeth. He was dressed as an officer but wore it as if he had simply tumbled out of bed; there was a loucheness about the way his dark blue frock coat was not neatly tucked and pressed, and it did not lie smoothly under his wide silver-laced dress belt, and the scarlet and silver waistcoat that poked from his neckline was uneven. Unlike the man on guard yesterday, he had no tall shako, but instead there was a smaller, red forage cap on the bar in front of him. His sash marked him as the officer of the regiment, but otherwise his stable-dress uniform was an everyday one, and quite unlike the pomp of the marching orders she was used to seeing on displays and parades.

But the thing that surprised Cordelia most about the gallant commanding officer was his age. Lizzie McNab had been in her very early twenties, a vivacious young woman who would have turned the head of any man. Captain Slatters was, quite clearly, a battled-hardened veteran of many years.

Cordelia stared, completely lost her cool, and blurted out, "Goodness, man, how old are you?"

He stared back, his eyes widening. He snorted, shook his head, looked down, and looked back up again.

She didn't say anything else. She was a lady and a

widow. She was allowed some leeway. She raised one eyebrow to try and brazen it out.

"I am forty-five, madam," he said eventually. "At least twice your age, I can see. Captain Percy Slatters, ancient of the regiment, at your service." He snatched up his forage cap, pressed it to his breast, and bowed very low and very slowly.

"I hope I have not offended you," she said. "I am Cordelia, Lady Cornbrook. I mention your age only because … I thought that soldiers retired from service after twenty years, or thereabouts. I am not sure. My military knowledge is sadly lacking."

"Allow me to educate you, then, my dear lady!" he said. As she waved her hand in acknowledgement, he grabbed it as if she had offered it to him, and pulled it to his lips, kissing the back of her glove gently. He let go after a second too long.

"Please do," she said, tucking both her hands into a fur muff and well away from his over-solicitous politeness.

"I am a man of the army, why, married to the army, I suppose you might say. Yes, I was there, my first real engagement; Waterloo, ah, the greatest battle of all time! Only as a drummer boy, then, mind, but oh, the smoke and the roar and the heroics, and it was then that I vowed my service to my country — for life!"

"How perfectly dramatic," she said, amused by his obviously well-rehearsed tale. Something in it didn't ring quite true but what did she really know of military matters? She filed it all away to ask someone about it, later.

She wasn't sure who.

Percy was speaking again. "Now, my dear lady, if you don't mind me prying — just a little — after all, you did mention my name, so might I ask, what is it that you want from me? For any service that I might be able to render shall be yours."

There was a laughing sparkle in his deep blue eyes and she wanted to like him very much. She was starting to see why Lizzie might have fallen for him, after all. Who didn't like a smart soldier with their shiny boots and drink-today-for-tomorrow-we-fight attitude? She said, "It is an awkward subject, I am afraid."

At that, he straightened up and nodded towards a booth. She followed him in and sat opposite. He leaned forward, knotting his weather-brown hands together as he bent to her full attention.

"You may say anything to me, my lady."

"Thank you. Did you know the girl who was murdered?"

He didn't react in any way surprised. He nodded. "Lizzie McNab," he said. "She is the talk of the town, now, the poor girl. And yes, I knew of her."

"*Of* her?"

She watched him closely. Was that a slight flush of the skin by his collar? He spoke steadily, though, with no waver of embarrassment in his voice. "Ahh, there are the rumours, are there not? I have read the papers. They make us out to be quite the couple! And yes, at one point, me and Lizzie, we walked out together, as it were. But look at me." He sat up straight and opened his hands wide. "I am a fighting man, as I said. I will be here this week and who knows? Gone the next! I am not a match for a sweet girl like her. Like she *was*. Ah… excuse me." He looked away, and blinked a few times. Cordelia wasn't sure if he was affecting emotion, or really felt it, but he didn't over-egg the display. He coughed and returned his attention to Cordelia. "But we were not lovers. Not in the … sense that they are saying."

"You weren't courting?"

"Goodness, no. Listen, I will tell you the truth. Don't believe the local rags. We spent a little time together, like folks do, but I had to tell her to go; it was not good for her reputation. She was of a good enough family, you know? *I* knew we could never have a future, but she was young, and they fall in love so easily, don't they?"

"Hold up one moment — so you are saying that Lizzie was infatuated with you, and you had to tell her to leave you alone?"

"In a manner of speaking. Yes, you have it right. Oh, but it was not so much of an event as you are making out. It was hardly even … well. Let us say that there are two sides in every story and I rather think she and I were reading different books."

"Hmm." Cordelia could not fight the rising suspicions she now had of dashing, gallant Percy. A lovelorn young girl, obsessed with an officer old enough to be her father; they had walked out, which would have been enough to encourage her. She would have followed him, plagued him, he would have grown tired of it and — there you had it, a perfect motive for murder.

"It doesn't look good for me, does it?" Percy said, as if he could follow her thoughts.

"No," she had to admit. "Save for the fact that you are still here, in this town. You haven't fled, and you seem to be talking openly."

"Seem," he repeated, and grinned. "Ah, well. The weather is bad, and anyway, where else would I be but with my regiment? I will assist Mr Gold and even that odious constable in their enquiries, but…"

"But what?"

He shrugged, and for a moment his face looked sad. It didn't suit him, and made him older than he was. "She was only a girl, with no family that is bothered to bring any prosecution. A good family, yes, but they had washed their hands of her, and not for any fault of hers. I rather think the authorities will let the matter drop, and quietly melt away by Christmas, and that will be the last we hear of it. And meanwhile the murderer is at large … no woman is safe."

"I hate to admit this, but I think you are right about the lack of care the authorities have." Cordelia rose to her feet. "Thank you for your time, Captain Slatters."

He rose too, and bowed, but as he came upright again, he fixed her with a very direct stare. "My lady, if I might be so bold to question you, now. What interest drives you to this case?"

"Oh." She decided she'd be as honest as she could. "She was my aunt's companion at Four Trees, and so I have a connection."

"Your aunt is Maude Stanbury?"

"Yes. Good day, sir."

She left, dashing past the frowning maid in the hallway.

I suppose everyone around here knows of Maude, she thought. *I suppose…*

* * *

Ruby was waiting for Cordelia at the bottom of the steps of the inn.

"I've just come from the garrison, my lady," she said. "And from what I heard there, you will have met Slatters within the inn."

"Indeed I have. First, though, what have you learned?"

"About Slatters, just that he has a woman in every town and a handful of babes for each woman besides."

"Ah." Cordelia glanced back at the blank windows of the inn. They reflected the daylight and did not allow those outside to look in. Shadows moved across the glass. "I am not terribly surprised. He said almost as much; he is certainly not the marrying sort."

"But I heard something more interesting than the captain's habits betwixt the sheets. They are saying that the doctor they called to examine Lizzie has changed his mind. Yes, she had opium in her body … but she *was* suffocated, just as one of the first doctors said."

Cordelia sighed. "And tomorrow morning, they will have yet another explanation. She will have been bitten by an asp or something."

"They seem most determined about this."

"Well, then. Does it make a difference, do you think? Killed is killed."

Ruby looked scornful. "It changes everything, my lady. It must have been a man to have done such a thing."

"What nonsense, and I am surprised to hear you say

that. I could suffocate a girl like that."

A couple walking past turned their heads when they overheard that, and scurried on a little bit faster. Ruby rolled her eyes and nodded to the waiting coach over the road, where Stanley was standing. "Er, my lady…"

"Indeed." Cordelia and Ruby picked their way across the cobbles and filth and reached Stanley, who was apparently in deep conversation with one of the horses.

He looked up, and his face was drawn and troubled. His stammer ebbed and flowed as he struggled to explain what was concerning him.

"What have you learned about Lizzie?" Cordelia asked.

"N-nothing, my lady, nothing at all."

"Then why are you so upset?"

Ruby snickered as she hauled herself into the carriage. "He probably saw someone's ankle and now he has to cut his own eyes out or something."

"Ruby! Enough." Cordelia knew her staff bickered amongst themselves but she did not expect to hear it in her presence. "Stanley, go on."

His bony shoulders twitched and he twisted his fingers in and around the leather reins. "I don't rightly know, for sure," he said in a low voice. "But something's coming. Something bad. Tonight or tomorrow night, they say, and I don't think they are talking about a rainstorm."

CHAPTER NINE

Cordelia felt Christmas fast approaching, and the weight of her aunt's disapproval lay heavy on her. Maude *knew* that Cordelia was looking into the death of Lizzie, she was sure of it. But they both continued their lying dance of duplicity in conversations.

It was Tuesday, and Cordelia had taken to her rooms. For most of the day, she had paced and thought and talked with Ruby. They wrote out their suspects on sheets of paper, and listed reasons why, and why not, they ought to be considered.

Percy Slatters was one, of course.

Iris, the silent, secretive dressmaker was another. Ruby couldn't fathom why Cordelia wanted to know more about her.

"They shared a room," Cordelia said. She was standing at the window, watching night fall early across the windswept moors. It was cold by the glass and a biting draught crept between the wood and the stone. "And there is another question that I have. Lizzie was Maude's companion, and a woman of gentle birth if not means. Why did she sleep up in the rafters with the servants? When I am old and doddery and need attending to, I shall have my companion sleep in a cot in my room."

"So that they may be at your beck and call," Ruby said. "What joy. For them."

"I am not going to end up like my aunt," Cordelia said. "I will not allow it. Indeed, I forbid it. And this does not answer my question."

"You ought to ask your aunt that."

"I suppose I must. But did Lizzie say nothing to you? You two were close, at least for the few days you knew her."

"Hardly close enough to discover each other's secrets," Ruby said. "Lizzie had always had that room up there, and all to herself. I simply think that Maude values her own space. When Iris arrived, she was put up there because Maude didn't trust her to be on her own. Lizzie didn't tell me about Percy. He is the most obvious suspect, you know."

"Especially now it was established she was poisoned *and* suffocated? That's another curious thing. Dead twice over. I wonder why?"

"I would not know how to poison someone," Ruby

said. "How much do you give them, to be sure of it?"

"Ah." Cordelia studied her own blurry reflection in the dark windowpane. Far in the distance, there was still a smudge of the red sunset. She turned to Ruby. "You might have something, there. Perhaps they intended to poison her but they did not give her enough, and she woke up."

Mistress and servant stared at one another. It felt very right, and Cordelia clicked her fingers as she walked over to where Ruby sat, surrounded by notes. "Write that down," she ordered. "We have it."

"We don't," Ruby protested.

"We have something."

Ruby sighed. Then she said, "What of that family that came here to ask your aunt for their boy's position in the mill? Lizzie was vile to them."

"She was. But foul enough for one of them to have lured her to the Ally Cross — or perhaps accidentally met her there — and killed her?"

Ruby closed her eyes. "No, no. I am wrong. I was people watching in the church that day. I saw them, I am sure of it."

"It is probably worth asking to check." Cordelia made a note. "Now, can you think of any motives that Iris would have had?"

"None at all, and I believe you are mistaken to consider

her a suspect."

"She is acting strangely, and that is enough for me," Cordelia said. "They clearly did not like one another."

"No one likes Iris."

"You must find out her history. She is with Maude today, is she not?"

"She is. Your aunt has her undertaking all manner of mending, and I for one cannot understand why she is submitting to it — Iris, I mean. She should have moved on by now."

"So, what keeps her here?"

Ruby shrugged. "She needs the money and has nowhere else to go. And it counts against her being the murderess because she would have left as soon as she could otherwise."

"I think she is clever, underneath it all. Fleeing causes suspicion."

"If we are talking of baseless, groundless suspicions, then that John Kitt is another unsavoury character. His politics are stirring but if I consider if from your point of view, he looks very suspicious."

Cordelia dismissed it. "Unlike Iris, he has no connection at all to the dead girl. Except that ... my aunt did say that he had given Lizzie some of his pamphlets. Was there more between them, do you think?"

Ruby threw her hands in the air and slapped them down on the notebook in her lap. She cried out in sudden frustration. "We know nothing, and this is all pointless, and I wish I'd never asked you to—"

Cordelia was about to interrupt and upbraid her servant for being so easy to dishearten, when they were both startled by a knocking at the door.

Maude burst in, leaning on a stick, and she stared around at the mess of paperwork.

Cordelia leaped to her side and helped her to the other wingback chair by the fire. Maude accepted, but she looked sniffily at Ruby, seated opposite her.

Ruby did not move until Cordelia narrowed her eyes at her. She flounced to her feet and began to gather up the notes littering the carpet.

"The cookery book is going well, then?" Maude said.

Cordelia wondered how good her aunt's vision was. Her eyes were watery but they fixed on a sheet of paper that had "Percy Slatters" written at the top, and underlined.

Perhaps Maude would simply assume Cordelia was back in the marriage market again. She crouched to snatch it up and make a pile of the papers, before taking the seat that Ruby had just vacated. Ruby went to the window but faced them, her hands folded before her, as if in an attitude of servantly waiting.

Cordelia knew she was simmering with her pent-up feelings. She ignored her.

"The cookery book is … ah, well, it has been so difficult to make progress. Your cook is … perfectly willing to talk, of course, but she's …" *Impossibly set in her ways and knows about ten dishes and all of them are dull.* Cordelia fanned the papers vaguely. "Well, you know. I think I shall write an article and send it to a ladies' journal."

"And you are interviewing local people, are you? I hope you keep to genteel places, and are always adequately chaperoned. I should not wish for bad words and rumours to make their way to my ears," Maude said warningly.

And indeed, that would not do. Cordelia would hate for her own flouting of social rules to affect her aunt. "I promise you I shall compromise my own name, but never yours," she said.

"Your name is mine, by degrees of connection, and you are under my roof." Maude worked her cheeks. "You have been in the inn in town."

"Ah. That. I was not in the public bar, of course. We took a room, did we not, Ruby?"

"With your servant of lowly birth," Maude added.

"I have no genteel companion," Cordelia said. "And Ruby suits me very well. Tell me, dear aunt, why did Lizzie sleep upstairs like a common servant, even before Iris came here?"

Maude's face was pulsating like a pair of bellows. "I took a companion at the insistence of my brother-in-law but in truth, she was more in the way than any comfort to me. It suited us both that she had her own space, and grateful she was for it, too. More than most would get." She harrumphed and waved her stick at the fire. "Sort that out. It's not drawing correctly."

Cordelia leaned forward and took the poker to the errant logs, shoving them together to stir up a fiercer flame. She glanced up at Ruby, who was still standing by the window.

The sunset had not yet disappeared.

In fact, it had only grown stronger.

"What on earth—"

Cordelia got to her feet and went to look through the glass. She smeared her sleeve over the cold pane.

Ruby turned, and drew in a sharp intake of breath. "The sky is red! What is happening?" Her hands twitched as if she wanted to cross herself.

"Fire," Cordelia said, and Stanley's dire warnings fell sharply into place. That way lay Simeon's factory. "Fire at the mill!"

Maude hauled herself to her feet and was at their side within an instant, clutching her stick as she wavered. She stared with them.

"Fire," she whispered throatily. "What do we do now?"

* * *

"Well, we don't stand around here like three old washerwomen," Cordelia said after a moment's thought. "Ruby, please take my aunt down to her sitting room and make her comfortable. I am going to find Stanley and Geoffrey and send them to render any assistance they can. People might be injured and if so … ah, Ruby, once Maude is settled, then come and find me there. We will need to turn Simeon's house into an infirmary if there are many wounded. It's the closest place."

"But—" both Maude and Ruby said at the same instant.

Cordelia whirled on them and fixed them in turn with her very best Withering Lady Stare.

They acquiesced immediately.

Cordelia snatched up a cloak and threw it around her shoulders as she left the room, leaving Ruby to her own task. In any other house, she would have changed to her indoor slippers but satin was not fit for keeping anyone's feet warm in this draughty pile, and she clattered along in her ankle-boots, grateful for the fur lining. She shot along the twisting, turning passages, ill-lit at erratic intervals by smoking lamps. The house seemed a lot larger on the inside when one was trying to get from one end to the other; she had a hunch that if she viewed a map of the place, the corridors would reveal themselves to be some kind of trick spiral, like in a novelty high-hedged maze.

She went first to the kitchen. When Stanley had arrived with them, he had been allocated a small room behind the stables. Maude had said it was so he could keep an eye on the horses, but as soon as they were out of earshot she told Cordelia it was because she'd have no men under her roof. And when Geoffrey had turned up, she had reiterated that command. "He's a shifty sort, is he not?" Maude had said.

"He is," Cordelia had been forced to confess.

Their room, especially with the two of them now in it, was uncomfortable and cold, and she knew they spent much of their time in the kitchen or the long servants' hall beyond it. And she was correct; they were both in the hall, warming themselves with soup and a small, but hot, fire.

"There is a fire at the mill," Cordelia said as she burst in. And inside, she sent up a little prayer of thanks that Geoffrey was here, and had clearly had no part in whatever insurrection was happening down there.

Both looked up, and Stanley looked shocked. "So that is what they meant!"

Geoffrey had not a hint of surprise on his face. Stanley got up but Geoffrey slurped his soup then put out a hand to tug the boy back to his seat.

"On your feet, both of you!" she ordered. "We need to go down immediately and see if any assistance is needed. There might be people trapped, or injured…"

"I doubt it," Geoffrey said laconically. "The main shift is over, and no lives will be lost."

"Why, then, there will be people fighting the fire, and you are needed for that!" she said. "That place is the only livelihood for many families hereabouts. Will you see them starve through lack of work?"

Stanley was pulling his jacket on even as she spoke. Geoffrey snarled something and remained seated. His insouciance was like a papercut to Cordelia's soul. She was so fired up that she strode over to him and dashed the soup bowl from his hand, hurling it with such force that it smashed against the far wall.

Silence fell.

Stanley stood in mute terror, his eyes large. Dark stains spread down the wall. Cordelia held her breath. She could not quite comprehend what she'd done.

She looked down at Geoffrey. He got to his feet, slowly, and did not meet her gaze. His tan face was flushed, she thought.

He cleared his throat. "I shall go down directly. Stanley, with me, boy. My lady, you stay here."

"No, I shall—"

"It will be no scene for a lady," he said, quietly and firmly.

She had won one battle and chose not to fight another. "Very well. Send word immediately if you have need of anything. Anything at all."

* * *

The cook and Kate had heard the noise and they poked their heads around the door to find Cordelia on her knees, picking up the shards of broken crockery. The cook descended on her in horror, her consternation at a lady doing such things sufficient to overcome her usual reticence.

"My lady! My lady, you must not! Kate—"

"At once," said the efficient maid. Cordelia was shooed to sit by the fire, where Ruby found her.

"Are we not going?" Ruby said. She was dressed for the outside now.

Cordelia outlined what had happened.

"You threw Geoffrey's soup against the wall?"

"I did. I can't believe it, but you know … it was rather fun."

Ruby tutted under her breath, and took a place on another bench by the table. Together, they waited for news from the mill, and ignored the cook's attempts to get Cordelia to join Maude in her sitting room.

It was always too cold up there, she thought, *and that's not because of the lack of heat.*

* * *

Cordelia itched with suspense. She desperately wanted to find out what was going on. Kate brought her hot cocoa and was persuaded to speak; she confirmed what Geoffrey had said, that the shift would be over. But no one knew anything more until at last, as the night was drawing towards ten o'clock, when Simeon came knocking at the front door.

Cordelia asked Ruby to go up to their rooms, see to warming her bed and nightclothes, and to turn in if she felt tired. She went to the sitting room to join her aunt and Simeon.

Simeon was dirty and dishevelled and his hands shook as he accepted a large glass of brandy from Maude. He flopped into the armchair and Maude retook the other seat. Cordelia perched herself on a sofa too far from the dying fire, but she was keen to hear what had happened.

"Thank you for sending your men," Simeon said firstly. "They have both rendered sterling assistance and I currently have one of my men doling out drink and hot food for them all."

Cordelia nodded. "But what happened? What of your mill?"

"The good news first; the main engine that runs the

110

mill is unharmed. Alas, two store sheds have gone up and are utterly destroyed. There is minor damage to a cutting floor, and also to a small kitchen area."

Maude could barely speak. She muttered something but she shook her head and rocked slightly to and fro.

"Was there any loss of life?" Cordelia asked. It seemed, to her, to be the most important thing.

"None, and I thank God for it," Simeon said. "There are some minor injuries, and that to the men fighting the fire. But no one is going to suffer long."

"Thank God indeed," Cordelia echoed.

Maude found her voice. "But the business. The business!"

Simeon nodded. "I cannot tell how bad this might be until the morning brings its light," he said. "Certainly we will not be running tomorrow, not even on short time, for a while. I am insured, of course."

"And what caused the fire, do you know?" Cordelia asked.

"What? *Who*, you mean…"

"Who," she said slowly, thinking of the mob and Stanley's foreboding.

"The constable arrived … eventually," Simeon said. He scowled, his usually genial face made unfamiliar and ugly. "He was drunk, the useless sot, and no help at all. But one of my men, my butler in fact, is a good sort and was incensed by this. He dunked the constable in a horse trough and fed him raw coffee until he was sick, and then he was a little more sensible. Together, they apprehended a boy." He turned his gaze to Maude, and said, "I believe a boy who is known to you. One from the town."

"To me? I know no boys! And certainly none from the town."

"It is a fact that those who engage in incendiarism will linger to watch their handiwork. And was it not in Keighley, not so long ago, that a farm labourer who had had his employ terminated for the winter season set alight all the barns of the farm? He claimed it was fair protest and his right as an Englishman, but he was still deported." Simeon drained his glass of brandy. Cordelia leaped to refill it. He continued, as she bustled to the decanter. "And so it was in this case. A young lad, dressed in rags, was found watching the conflagration from a hiding place on the hill above the mill, and he did not deny it; he only cried about his work, or lack of it. Apparently he had been laid off recently, and his family had come to me to plead his case, and I had sent them away. You did not tell me, dear Maude, that this family had come also to you."

Cordelia passed him the fresh tumbler of alcohol, and retook her seat. "Indeed? The family that came here that

112

stormy night, Maude, you remember."

The old woman was exhausted with the long night. Her eyelids half-drooped and she looked fed up with everything. She sighed heavily. "And so he turned to spite and fire-setting, did he? And what did he think to gain by that? The poor are poor because they are so stupid."

"Maybe the poor are poor because…" But Cordelia let herself trail off. What, was she herself a Chartist now? Simeon fixed her with a curious stare, but it flickered for only a moment. He was curled over himself with tiredness, now. She decided not to ask after the fate of the boy. Instead, she got heavily to her feet. "Simeon, do you rest here tonight? I shall direct a room to be made up." She said that for her aunt's sake. In truth, she would do it herself, with Ruby gone to bed and Kate likely the same.

Luckily, Simeon shook his head, and said his coach waited outside. They took one another's leave, and soon the house was dark and quiet once more.

113

CHAPTER TEN

It was a gut-wrenchingly sad scene. Cordelia found that she could go no further, not immediately. She stood on a small rise above the mill and looked down at the charred, blackened heaps that were being piled up in the yard outside the buildings. One of those buildings had no roof and the tops of the walls were a jagged, black crenulation of broken and damaged bricks.

The early morning sunlight cast a misty, pale glow on everything, making things seem ghostly and the air was strangely still.

"It is the smell," Ruby said, holding a handkerchief to her nose. "I think that's the worst."

"Yes." A mixture of wood, brick, cloth and something unnameable assailed her nostrils. She watched for another moment longer before picking her way down the rocky slope.

They had walked from Four Trees, accompanied by Stanley who was carrying a large hamper of food for the workers. Kate and the cook had toiled since before dawn. Cordelia wondered how much sleep the white-faced maid of all work got, and how long it would be before she sought a better position elsewhere — or turned to the mill for employment. At least she would have Sundays off, there.

Geoffrey was already there. According to Stanley, he had stayed the night. Cordelia suspected that Simeon's butler's free alcohol might have had something to do with that. She saw her black-clad coachman at a distance. He was carrying a large beam of wood from the shattered building, limping very slightly, and did not seem to see her.

Ruby and Stanley took the hamper of food into one of the mill's surviving rooms. Cordelia spotted Simeon, and made her way towards him.

"And in the cold light of day," she said, "how does it look now?"

He smiled weakly, rubbing his smut-marked face with a cloth. He was still smart and dandyish, but his white cuffs were grubby and his face showed cares and strains. "It will be an expensive job to fix quickly, or a cheap job to fix more slowly. However, the cheap option is false economy, of course, because the more swiftly I can return the mill to a full working order, the sooner we begin to make money once more."

"Ah," she said. "I imagine then that you will take the expensive course."

"I shall, indeed." He sighed. "I have some stocks I might sell and capital I can release. Ah, business." He waved his hand, still holding the cloth. "It is nothing for you to fret about. The mill shall survive. In fact, I shall use the chance to make improvements. I thought I might build a classroom, you know. Attach a school. And a dormitory."

"Whatever for?"

"There are many poor orphans in the land, especially in London, and Manchester. The workhouses there are full of them. What a waste! I could offer them something here, as apprentices."

"That sounds almost philanthropic."

"Indeed. They would work, of course, and that would be good for them and their souls. I see it as profitable all round."

"You'd pay them?" she asked.

"Not as apprentices, below the age of sixteen, of course not, no. They would be paid in free food, and somewhere to live, and schooling, and discipline. They would gain self-respect and a work ethic and a strong soul. Such things are invaluable."

Cordelia nodded. "It could work."

"Others are doing something similar," he said. "I particularly wish to model myself on Mr Greg's efforts in Cheshire."

Cordelia knew nothing of that but she smiled encouragingly. "And I should imagine that this will satisfy the agitators, too?"

"No; I don't think anything will make those demons happy. They don't want work yet they do want to vote, and they wish to shake up parliament so that we don't know who is who and what is what and how to be or any such thing. That John Kitt is a malign influence and you know, I was sorry when we caught that boy who set this fire."

"Sorry?"

Simeon looked around. "Yes. I was hoping it would be revealed that Kitt did this, and then we could hang him and be done with it all. Without him here, stirring folks up, none of this would have happened. And now people are scared and hysterical and they hardly know what they are scared of — not to mention a murderer on the loose, as the papers like to constantly remind us! Why, that might be Kitt too. I would believe it of him."

"Why do you think Kitt might have killed Lizzie, though? There would surely have to be a motive beyond sheer spite. Do you know of any connection between them?" She tried to sound conversational.

"A connection, yes, so I understand. I saw him speaking to her, and to the other one, that silent seamstress also, one day when I came to call on Maude. I chased him off, I can tell you. He had no right to be on Maude's land, spreading his poison."

"Really? He spoke to both girls?" She knew he'd spoken with Lizzie; but Iris, too?

"Spoke … and more, I shouldn't wonder," Simeon said darkly. "He has a way with women, especially young ones, with all that evil charm, and no manner of ethics — ah! Forgive me!" He suddenly flushed and took a step backwards. "This is not a conversation we should have, dear Cordelia. It is strange," he added. "Sometimes I forget who you are and simply talk to you as if you…"

"As if I were just a normal person?"

"As if you were a man."

"Exactly what I said," she retorted pertly, but softened it with a smile. "I should let you get on — ah! The regiment approaches."

Along the track came a troop of marching men, not in smart battle dress but in their stable order, ready to help out with whatever they could do. At the head of the men on foot rode Percy Slatters, and he was dressed finely, clearly marking him as both a man of substance, and a man who did not intend to get himself dirty.

Percy hailed them, and Cordelia took herself to a discreet distance as Simeon went to converse with the yeomanry.

Cordelia soon grew bored. Everyone around her had an appointed task and was working smartly and efficiently. She had seen the devastation for herself, but even as she watched, she could see superficial improvements. Of course, the larger task of restoring some of the engines would take longer, but already a black-clad man in a tall top hat with a roll of papers under his arm was now being shown around by Simeon. He looked like a gentleman-engineer, and was no doubt assisting in the plans for rebuilding.

She was looking for Ruby, to tell her she wanted to return to Four Trees, when she spotted the constable approaching, and he was accompanied by the magistrate in the area, William Gold.

Well, she corrected herself, *he is no magistrate, so I have learned. He is a Justice of the Peace, apparently.* In an earlier conversation, Maude had said that she thought he was one of the finest men around, and a very prominent landowner. Simeon had remarked that he was very good at raising the finance for road building though the standard of the roads led Cordelia to wonder where that finance had gone.

No one had made any comment on his law skills,

however, and as a JP he didn't need any. London was now bringing in stipendiary magistrates who had to study legal matters, but up here in the wild north, no one cared — even if they had heard of the practise, which most had not. People called him "magistrate" or "justice" or "JP" or mostly, just "Mr Gold."

He looked like everyone's favourite uncle. He had a pinkish face and cheeks like apples, and grey whiskers that fluffed at the edges, soft and fuzzy. He was dressed in sober blacks, unlike Simeon's dandy colours and the constable's shades of working-man's-brown.

William Gold nodded at Simeon and the engineer, but made a beeline for Cordelia, sinking low in a bow and taking her hand very gently in his. "My lady," he said, in a rich and melodious voice. "First, I am full of apologies for my unforgiveable indecorous behaviour."

"Mr Gold, do not trouble yourself," she said. "I am not aware of any such behaviour."

"Oh, my lady, the fact that I have not called upon you while you have been staying with the incomparable Miss Stanbury," he said. "And when I had a chance — when I was in the area — well, that was such a sad business, and I was rather busy."

Ah yes, he had been at Four Trees when Lizzie had been found dead, but she had not spoken to him; only with his lecherous constable. She had noticed him, and he was easy to recognise again. She reassured him that everything was in order and no offence had been taken. "But," she pressed on, "what progress are you making, if I might ask? I would rather you ignore all the social propriety in the world if you are in the pursuit of a murderer!"

"Oh, the girl was silly to be up there at the Ally Cross," he said, and suddenly he didn't look so avuncular. "With a man, too, most likely. She was young and beautiful. Such girls attract men, and are too silly to know what to do with them."

Cordelia frowned and drew herself up tall. "Silliness is still no reason for anyone to be killed," she said, "or else I should be dead many times over already."

"I am sure you are not in the habit of allowing yourself to be seduced by any rough sort of man with a silver tongue," he said.

"Even so," Cordelia said. "What if this man, this rough sort, silver tongue and all, finds another young girl? What if he kills again? I cannot imagine the murderer would be content with one, now he has a feel for it."

"Then the girls of this parish need to take heed, and stay at home, and bide with their families. It is a lesson, don't you think?" he said. He plastered a very patronising smile onto his face. She wanted to poke a sharp stick into his fleshy apple cheeks now. "Now, I can see you are a lady of some passion yourself, but let me give you some advice. The people of this parish are an untamed sort, and need some direction — firm direction. I keep the peace here, and I am responsible for the Commission hereabouts which seeks to bring improvement. Roads, and bridges, and all that business. Now, look there: Mr Welsh will rebuild, and he will rebuild a better engine, do you see? Some things need to be lost … destroyed … before they can be renewed. As it is in society, my good lady."

A sharp stick? Cordelia's fingers twitched. Maybe she could pull one of her hatpins free. But she was a lady — as his words reminded her — and she had a place, and a face to present, and a set pattern to follow.

She would scream into her pillow later. But for now, she allowed herself a small and humourless smile, the very minimum that politeness dictated. She wasn't done with her questions but she changed the subject. "And what of the mill?" she asked. "There was a boy arrested, I understand…"

"Mm, yes. A poor starving mite."

"So the courts will be lenient?"

The Justice tipped his hat to her, and waved his cane towards Simeon, hailing him. He half-turned back to Cordelia before he walked away. "Of course not. What sort of message would that send?"

* * *

Cordelia found Ruby and her other servants. Geoffrey was sweat and dirt-stained, and she thanked him profusely for his efforts. He shrugged it off, but accepted her direction to return to Four Trees with Stanley and to take some rest.

"Ruby, we will tour round and thank each worker ourselves, and then make our way home too."

"Why is it down to us to thank these people?" Ruby muttered. "We are not part of this mill."

"I am family, loosely, to Simeon, and furthermore he does not have a female in his house who can perform this office. So I feel that it falls to us. This is what is done, Ruby. It is the role of women. You are still learning to be a lady's maid, and I know it is a world unfamiliar to you."

"Well, take on a posher sort as your maid, then," she said grumpily. "You cannot make me into the type that you want. I am who I am."

"True," Cordelia said. "Only you can make yourself into something better. Come."

They worked their way around the site, though no one seemed terribly bothered or grateful for Cordelia's thanks. They did not take long. It was only ten minutes before Cordelia relented and said to Ruby, "We are done. Let us

— ah! Now, why do you think that she is here?"

Down the track, towards the mill, walked Iris the seamstress, with her mousey hair unbound and cascading around her face, and her long cloak streaming out behind her.

To Cordelia, she looked like a painting of Cassandra.

Ruby said, "This is just the sort of place that the creepy woman would be, isn't it? And she doesn't look like she's quite right..."

* * *

People didn't usually notice Iris but they certainly did at this moment, as she strode into the centre of the courtyard. The soldiers had cleared the damaged buildings and made piles of the rubbish, sorting them into wood, and stone, and metal. All could be salvaged in some way, and re-used. She spun around slowly, and tipped her head back, sniffing the air like a wild animal, her large pixie eyes half-closed.

Cordelia was captivated. "Do you think she is drunk or something?" she whispered to Ruby.

"I think something is influencing her, for certain," Ruby hissed back.

Iris fully closed her eyes, and she licked her pale lips with a tongue that was shockingly pink against her pallid skin.

The soldiers stared. William Gold, Simeon and the engineer were somewhere within the building, out of sight and earshot, but Percy took charge. He broke the spell, and marched over to the uncanny-looking seamstress.

He grabbed her elbow, and bent to whisper something in her ear.

"Oh," Ruby said. "Does he know her?"

"I doubt it… why?"

"She is looking at him, now. See how she looks at him. That is … familiarity."

Iris leaned against the captain. He put an arm around her shoulder, but his knuckles were white, and he led her very forcefully towards Cordelia and Ruby.

"Miss Fletcher has been quite overcome with emotion," he said through thinned lips. "Lady Cornbrook, I am sorry to impose on you … but I know she resides currently at your aunt's house … she is friendless, quite alone in the world and I wonder if you might …"

"Of course," Cordelia said, thinking, *yes, Ruby is correct; he knows her, or at least knows of her. He knows her name and place.* "We shall see her safely back to Four Trees."

Iris's slate-grey eyes flew open and looked beyond them. Cordelia glanced over her shoulder but there was nothing there but the morning mist burning away in the weak winter sunlight. Iris said, in a voice like a cavern's

126

echo, "Friendless? There is a lie; none of us are friendless."

Cordelia looked at Ruby, startled. Already Percy was hurrying away from the scene, leaving it to the women to sort out. But, if Iris was in an uncharacteristically communicative mood, this might be useful, Cordelia thought. "Who are your friends, that we might contact them for you, Iris?" She spoke carefully, as if to a child or one who was unwell in the mind.

"I am surrounded by them right now," Iris whispered.

Ruby was frowning, and Cordelia thought that Iris didn't mean either of them. "Who?" she insisted.

Iris clasped her hands together and pressed them to her chest. Under the cloak she was only wearing a long linen gown, well-made but of rough and homely material. She let her head incline to one side, and sighed deeply. "All of our ancestors surround us and watch us," she said. She was still gazing into nothingness. "See, there, and there, and there… and we have angels, too, sent by the Lord to protect us."

Ruby was openly rolling her eyes but Cordelia sent her a fierce look. To Iris, Cordelia said, as kindly as she could, "That may be, but we also ought to take care to protect ourselves on this earth. Come, let us return to Four Trees."

But Iris discovered a burst of energy and strength that took them both by surprise, and flung herself away from them, running up to stand on a charred beam of wood that

Geoffrey had laid out in the yard earlier. She said, "I have all the protection I need. I am protected by spirits, you see."

"Brandy, more like," Ruby muttered.

"Hush, slattern. Iris, Iris, dear girl, do step down and come along with us. It has been so very trying … the loss of Lizzie, the dreadful circumstances. You must not read the newspapers. They stir up fear."

Iris looked confused for a moment. "I never read the newspapers. Why would I? I have all the information that I need … within. And anyway, oh, that silly Lizzie … well …"

"Well what?" Cordelia said, her voice hardening as she stepped closer and looked up at the dreamy-faced seamstress. "You said before that you knew nothing of Lizzie, though you shared a room. What did you not say? What do you know?"

Iris blinked and finally met Cordelia's eyes. They were still glazed and unearthly but Cordelia had the sense that Iris was, at last, perceiving reality once more.

Though if she was only now seeing reality, what was she looking at before? Visions? Or delusions?

"I know nothing. I didn't know her," Iris said, and she was back to her normal, stubbornly uncommunicative self once more. She stepped down from the log and looked around, shrinking in on herself, and clutching the cloak

128

tightly closed. "She was a woman who did have friends. She could laugh like a lady. I'm nobody, and can tell you nothing."

"Do you know who *her* friends were?" Cordelia said.

Iris shook her head very quickly, burrowing her chin into her cloak. "Not for me to say, my lady, forgive me, excuse me. They were …" She swallowed, deeply. She rolled her eyes, and it made her look cagey. With an apparent effort she said, "they were mostly men, if you get my meaning. She walked out … with many men."

And then she was gone, scurrying out of the courtyard like a frightened deer. As she left, she cannoned into another woman who was entering, and sent her ricocheting off the stone gate pillar. The woman raised her fist and shouted something obscene after the retreating figure, but Iris did not look back.

"Do you believe that?" Cordelia said to Ruby. For herself, she did not believe a word of it. What did that mean? Iris was hiding something. "Do you believe that Lizzie had many men, and not just…" She nodded towards Percy, and was immediately caught by the sight of a fresh scene. Percy was not looking towards them.

He was staring at another approaching woman, and he did not look happy.

* * *

"Get back to work!" Percy snapped at his lounging

soldiers. He hurried forward to intercept the woman who was bearing down on him with a face like thunder.

"So I find you at last," she cried out, in an accent more of the north-east than the north riding of Yorkshire. "They tried to fob me off at your headquarters but I tracked you here, and then they mocked me at the garrison but I will not be put off, oh no!"

"Delilah, Delilah, you are a vision, as always…"

"Oh, get away with your honeyed words! I'll have none of it. Two bairns you've left me with ——two!"

"But Delilah, that cannot be, for I was only there a few months…"

"Two at once, you bone-headed idiot! Twins! Trust me to fall for a man quite so … inconveniently *virile*. And now you must pay for them, for the parish'll not keep me."

Ruby was grinning, but she nodded towards the gate. "Come, my lady. Entertaining though this is, I fear it might descend into something ignoble. You think I am not aware enough of polite society but I do know we ought not to be here."

"You are correct." Cordelia gathered her skirts in one gloved hand to keep them clear of the ash and dirt. "Let us get back to Four Trees. I think I have learned enough to take the investigation forward, you know."

"How so?"

"Mm. A lot has just occurred. Let me ponder it a while."
Ruby sighed, and trailed behind.

CHAPTER ELEVEN

On Thursday, Cordelia was surprised to find Stanley and Iris in conversation in the small yard outside the back of the house. It was a sheltered area between the scullery and the back kitchen door, with a rough slate roof though it was open to the elements on one side. Light rain pattered on the slates. Just beyond the cover, there were a few pots which gave evidence of a straggling herb garden there in the summer months. Iris was scrubbing a piece of fabric, kneeling down on some cloth to protect her knees as she bent over the small metal bath. Stanley was standing very erect, and looking wild-eyed and upset.

Conversation? No, it was an argument, Cordelia corrected herself. "Stanley, I was hoping you could drive me into town. We can just take Maude's light gig. She hardly uses it."

"Of course." He looked relieved and jumped to his

task. Cordelia lingered for a moment, but Iris's bowed head and furious scrubbing told her that she would not be talking. She withdrew to the sitting room to stay warm while Stanley prepared the gig.

"Has that daft girl finished laundering that gown yet?" Maude demanded.

"She appears to still be working. She is very conscientious."

"She is not. She is a waste of my time and money. If she got things right the first time, she would have been long gone from here by now."

Was Iris deliberately making mistakes, Cordelia wondered idly. Yet Iris had been packing and talking of leaving — what had happened there to make her stay? And knowing Maude's pernickety nature, nothing Iris did would be good enough. Cordelia could see from how her aunt treated the cook and Kate that she was never satisfied. A servant had to accept that they would always be sub-par.

If you didn't accept, Cordelia thought, *then you'd be doomed to try and fail forever. If Iris didn't make a stand, she'd be altering Maude's dresses on her deathbed.*

The gig was ready. She made a vague excuse to Maude and hurried out to meet Stanley.

"What were you two arguing about?" she asked as soon as she saw him again.

134

"We weren't arguing, my lady," he stammered, his red face telling another story.

"What were you *talking* about, then?"

"Her soul and its certain damnation," Stanley said with such a morose tone that Cordelia had to bite her lip to stop her smile.

"Surely all are saved," she said. "I saw her with a Bible, you know."

Stanley shook his head and helped Cordelia up in to the gig. He pulled the cover up and over and passed her a blanket to tuck around her knees. It wasn't the best vehicle for bad weather, but the rain was light, and she didn't really think the short journey justified using more than one horse.

He climbed up to the seat alongside her, making sure not to let his clothing touch hers. He was very correct in his manner, and she knew he would find it hard to speak in the way that she wanted. She let him drive them along in silence.

As the gig bounced and jolted over the track, she thought through her plan. She was intrigued by Percy and knew that he held the key to the unlocking of Lizzie's secrets. It was going to be a difficult conversation, but she wanted to ask him if he knew of any other lovers that Lizzie might have had.

Stanley drew up by the inn, and helped her down. She

gave him some coin to see to the horse, and himself if he wanted a pie, and went straight up into the saloon bar, hoping to see Percy where she had seen him before.

But he was not there, and the maid in the hallway caught up with her. "My lady," she said, meaningfully. "Do come to a room."

"Thank you; might you tell me if Captain Slatters has been seen in here today?"

"No, my lady, he has not. This way, if you please."

"Ah, thank you. But I must go."

Cordelia escaped the maid's grasp. Now the rumours would be that Lady Cornbrook was indulging in a scandalous and ruinous affair with a Captain of the Hussars, and part of her was rather amused.

She hoped, though, that neither Maude nor her staff got to hear of it.

She left the inn and paused at the top of the steps. Stanley was turned away, watering the horse, as he did not expect her out so soon. She looked around, and caught the dark eye of John Kitt. Her stomach tightened.

He was leaning casually against the wall at the base of the steps, and looking up at her. His face had not been shaved in a few days, and his strong chin was darkly shadowed to match his curling hair. His black hat was set at an angle on his head, and he smiled very slowly.

"My lady Cornbrook," he said.

"How do you know who I am?"

"You know who *I* am."

"Do I?"

"Of course you do. I can see it in your face."

"Are you some kind of mesmerist or mind-reader?"

"Not at all. But there is curiosity and fear in your eyes, and I cannot imagine you would have either emotion when you look at the usual sort of lowly working man such as myself. But I can imagine that you feel those things when faced with the notorious John Kitt." He plucked his hat from his head and bowed in a shallow and insulting way. "At your service."

"I thought you didn't hold with such things," she said. "Service, and the like. I have seen you talk. Preach, I suppose, is more accurate a description. You rail against the natural order of things and want to destroy it all."

"Not quite all," he said, smiling and showing his teeth wolfishly. He had a strong voice, gravelly, with a hint of accent. *Was he an educated man, or not*, she found herself wondering.

"What do you know of the fire at the mill?" she said, hoping her challenge would catch him off guard and force a revelation from his expression, if not his words.

But he didn't waver. "I hear only that it was swiftly

contained, and that a boy has been caught for it, the poor starving mite."

"Perhaps he was not acting alone. Perhaps he was *incited*."

Kitt lifted one shoulder in the slightest of insouciant shrugs. "As to that, I cannot say." Suddenly he uncoiled, like a released spring, and darted up the stone stairs so that he now stood but two steps below her. He dug one wide hand into his jacket and withdrew some leaflets, much like the ones that he had disseminated at the church, and that Ruby had taken to read.

"Would you like to know what I truly oppose?" he said in a thrillingly low voice, so that she had to fight the urge to bend forward to hear him. She forced her back ramrod-straight and looked down her nose at him.

"No, I—"

"Hoi! You, there!"

Cordelia jumped, and put a hand to her throat as if she had been caught in the act of stealing. The constable was walking briskly towards them, and he was waving his hand in their direction. "Hoi!" he called again. "Kitt! You have been warned about distributing your seditious literature and pamphlets and so forth. This time, I shall call the yeomanry on you, yes I shall! And menacing a lady, too, why…"

"Are you feeling menaced, my lady?" Kitt whispered,

his eyes never leaving hers. He ignored the approach of Kennett completely.

"Yes," she said, then, "no, of course not; I am *never* menaced. Goodness, no." She stepped backwards towards the sanctuary of the inn.

He hesitated, as if he were going to pursue her. She remembered kicking Hugo Hawke down the stairs, and gathered herself to repeat the movement. But then she had been wearing a summer ball-gown, light and airy. In her heavy winter skirts and petticoats and crin-au-lin, she did not think she could get her leg higher than six inches with any force.

There was no need. Kennett was now labouring up the steps, and Stanley was fast behind him, every sinew in his young man's body vibrating with indignation that his mistress was apparently being threatened.

Kitt laughed. He tucked the papers back inside his jacket even as he turned and took a light leap onto the wall that bordered the steps. One more jump, and he was the other side, and running down the street with a long, easy lope. She was certain that she heard him laughing as he went.

Kennett cursed, and Stanley muttered, "There is a lady present," and Kennett cursed again to show Stanley he cared nothing for the young man's criticism.

Kennett said, "That man, and his dissention and his pamphlets, why, he has been reported for it before by that poor maid, and called up to account for it, and directed to leave this place, and yet here he is …"

Cordelia swept past the constable before he could get into full flow. "Thank you, Stanley," she said to her coach boy. "I can always rely on you. Shall we go on?"

"This way, my lady."

CHAPTER TWELVE

Cordelia had no luck in trying to find Percy to talk to him. She spent the day trudging around the town in the increasingly heavy rain, chaperoned by Stanley, until both were fed up and miserable. He drove her back to Four Trees in silence, where she found that Simeon had been invited for dinner. He stayed late, and was congenial company. Even though she was exhausted by the time she got to bed, she did not feel as if she slept at all.

And the next morning, Maude too complained of poor sleep. "Ever since this dreadful business," she remarked, buttering some cold toast with precision. "Ever since … I wake in the night, now, tossing and turning."

"Oh, dear aunt," Cordelia said. "Maybe it is time, for your own peace of mind, to consider moving in with Simeon."

"No. This is my house."

Cordelia had expected the objection. "Then, at the least, it would be wise for you to place a notice in the paper calling for a new companion. I know you are not keen, but it makes sense. You cannot be alone here. Indeed, I do not want to leave you while this is all so unresolved."

"Nonsense. You have to get back to your own house, as you keep telling me."

"I will, soon. Before Christmas, I assure you. But there are things I am doing here … ah, the book, you know. The article, I mean."

"You are not really doing the cookery thing, are you?" Maude said.

Cordelia skirted the issue. "The plain fact is, that I cannot go while you are alone here. And no, neither Kate nor the cook count."

"There is Iris. I could make her stay."

"Make? No, aunt, you could ask, but do you think she is a suitable companion?"

Maude would not meet Cordelia's eyes. She ate her way silently through two rounds of toast. Cordelia let the matter drop, but resolved to take it up with Simeon. It worried her, the thought of Maude being alone in the remote house, especially with her recent insomnia problems.

After breakfast, Maude retreated to her private study. Cordelia hoped it was to draft a notice for the newspapers asking for a new companion. She left her aunt to it, and went instead to seek out Iris. Since the young woman's strange appearance at the mill, things had been preying on Cordelia's mind.

It was a clear day, the rain having petered out overnight, but it was bitterly cold. The corridors could have stored ice in them. Cordelia walked briskly through the twisting passageways; they were uncarpeted and the cold seemed to seep even through her boots. She clattered up the stairs to the rooms under the eaves.

"Iris?" she called as she made her way to the half-open door. Iris had consistently refused invitations to complete her sewing in a downstairs room. Maude had wanted her in the servants' hall, where she would be close by if Maude needed her, and also warm by the fire. Instead the seamstress had stubbornly remained upstairs, citing that she needed peace and that she did not want the fine fabrics to be contaminated by the soot and food smells.

Cordelia was more and more suspicious of Iris. No travelling seamstress she had ever known had taken quite so long, not even when engaged in the making of dresses for a family of debutantes.

And her suspicions exploded further when she reached the door, and knocked, and pushed it open, to reveal the room's sudden and stark emptiness.

Iris had left.

* * *

Cordelia did not go to Maude. She went, instead, straight to Stanley, and found him in the servants' hall. This trip away was something of a holiday for him, and she didn't mind him taking an hour or two out of his day to read a book, as he had worked so hard at the mill helping to clear up with Geoffrey.

Thinking then of Geoffrey, she first asked where he was.

"Attending to the coach, my lady," he said. "There was a problem with the axle. It has suddenly happened, apparently. I did not notice a problem before."

"Does he not need your help?"

"I tried, my lady." Stanley began to stammer in embarrassment. "And then he sent me away, saying I made matters worse."

"Ah." She pulled a bench away from the table and sat down carefully on the edge of it. The sheer volume of her skirts were starting to make movement awkward. "Will you speak to me frankly, Stanley? I have just discovered that Iris Fletcher has left, and no one knew anything about it, so she must have gone in the night. Had you heard?"

His face showed that he had not heard. "My lady, no, nothing. But she barely speaks when she joins us for meals here. She did eat dinner with us last night."

"Yet you were speaking to her earlier in the day. You said it was about her damnation. Tell me more, Stanley."

Haltingly, he explained that Iris professed to be a Christian, but it was soon obvious that it was not the sort of traditional branch of the religion that he approved of. Indeed, she claimed to have angels sitting on her shoulder and speaking to her. She believed in fairies, and demons, and spirits, "and all manner of evil stories," Stanley said. "It is a twisted and wrong sort of faith, I think. She cannot see how seduced she is by the Evil One."

Cordelia wondered what difference there was between God talking to you and a spirit or angel, but she did not voice it. It would distress the devout young man far too much, and anyway, it was not a question she was overly concerned with. "She does sound troubled," she commented mildly. "Does she attend any services that you know of?"

"Not locally, no, but she did refer to a place in a previous town. Spiritists, they were, and she spoke of destiny, and said she had seen proof that we live again and again, the same soul in new bodies." He shuddered. "I would not hear more. I closed my ears to it, and thought of Heaven, my lady."

"Destiny. That's something I've never had much time

for," Cordelia said, half to herself. "I have always made my own way. Now, here is another odd thing. A week ago, she was packing to leave. Yet she did not go. I fancied, at the time, that I had persuaded her to stay. But now I wonder if I flatter my powers rather too much. I wonder if there was another reason?"

Stanley looked blank. "I know not, my lady. I can think of no reason she stayed, and no reason she has gone now — save for the fact that Miss Stanbury is a hard taskmaster."

"Indeed she is, and perhaps the most obvious solution is the correct one. Iris has simply had enough, and she has gone."

"But in the night … she would not have been paid."

Cordelia stared. "Oh no; she would not. Well, I think it is time I told my aunt about this, and also asked her to check the house's valuables in case Iris thought to take her payment in some other means."

She stood up and made herself ready. This was not going to be an easy conversation.

CHAPTER THIRTEEN

The sudden disappearance of Iris caused consternation in the household, and Maude directed every cupboard and drawer to be opened out and itemised. She spent the day in making lists and collating information, searching for a missing button or a lost book that she might accuse the seamstress of theft.

"I knew it!" she muttered. "They are all the same…"

But nothing seemed to be amiss. The dresses and gowns and mending were all laid out in an upstairs drawing room, a cold and dark place that was never used. They had been arranged on the backs of chairs and across small tables, and in the gloom they seemed to be like ghosts. Cordelia shivered and gathered them up to take to Maude's dressing room.

Maude herself prowled and poked and lifted and assessed and found everything satisfactory, which seemed to cause her the most pain of all.

She sent for Mr Gold, who arrived that evening, and they dined together with Simeon present again as well. The Justice expressed his concern that a potential suspect had disappeared.

"I thought you were saying it was a man, and a lover of Lizzie, that had done the deed?" Cordelia said.

Mr Gold did not like being contradicted. He stabbed his fork into a slice of chicken. "Of course. But the nature of investigations is a fluid one, you know. This new information makes that young girl look very suspicious indeed. No one leaves in the night, without taking the pay that is owed to them, if they have nothing to hide. So now I am reconsidering my earlier suspicions."

"That does sound very reasonable and sensible," Cordelia admitted. "So you will look closely into the matter?"

He chewed slowly for a while before saying, "We shall not waste *too* much time on it. If it was a lover, then my earlier opinions still stand: it is a warning to other flighty girls. And if it was the seamstress, then she is gone. The main thing is to establish if anything has been taken from Miss Stanbury."

Theft of a rich person's property ranked as more important than the death of a friendless young woman. Cordelia drew in a long, ragged breath. The man was impossible. Was it ineptitude or sheer laziness? It would have been different if it had been a man of means that was killed. The unfairness burned her. She took a gulp of wine. "I understand that you are an awfully busy man," she said carefully. "Maybe if the county were to raise a police force, then…"

They all spluttered with indignation — Maude, Simeon and Mr Gold alike.

"No, no, no," Mr Gold said eventually as his chortles subsided. "That simply won't do. I am aware that London is trying it out, but no good can come of it. We will have no French spies up here, mark my words!"

"They are not French, nor are they spies," she protested. "I understand that the system is working very well in London, and other places also."

"I heard they are nothing more than lobsters," Simeon said, smiling. "They may look blue, but as soon as they get into hot water — oh, they will turn red, and become as soldiers, you shall see."

It was a phrase she had heard before and she understood the sentiment. Before she could speak, Mr Gold cut in again.

"No," he was saying. "The English way is quite different. We can take care of ourselves. We do not need these policemen to tell us what to do. The thought makes me ill."

"Not to mention the expense," Maude said, her eyes glittering. "Taxes will rise, and for what? So that we might pay for our own oppression. No. I am utterly opposed."

"As are all right-thinking folk," Mr Gold assured her. He beamed around the table. "At least we all agree."

"I—" Cordelia said, but Mr Gold reached over and patted her hand with a too-familiar air, the prerogative, she thought of older married men with such status.

Still, she withdrew her hand sharply.

"You are still learning about our ways," he said, patronisingly. "Ah! More wine!"

Talk turned to toll roads, and she simmered away to herself.

* * *

Mr Gold said that he was directing his constable to work with the soldiers at the garrison to look for Iris Fletcher, but it was a half-hearted affair. No hue and cry was raised. Indeed, it seemed to be treated by the yeomanry as a day out and they ambled through the town in the light drizzle, simply stopping passers-by at random and saying, "Have you seen Iris?" Most people did not know who Iris was, and went on quickly. The soldiers tried to describe her, with desultory results. "She's about average height, and normal looking. But with bigger eyes."

Cordelia sat in the gig, with the rain pattering on the roof. It was cold as the cover was a folding one that came down, clam-shell-like, to hover over the occupant's head but it afforded no protection from the sideways wind. She had asked Stanley to drive her to town again in her search for Percy, but she was told that he was "out on the search."

"We ought to search, too," she said, "but with more direction. Why do they ask here? She is unlikely to be in this town. She will go to where she was last, or has friends or family."

She remembered that she'd heard Iris had no family. *The poor girl*, she thought. *No wonder she seeks connection in other ways, and wants to talk to the dead.*

"Let's return to Four Trees," Cordelia said at last. Stanley slapped the reins on the chestnut's rump and the gig lurched forward. "Stanley, tell me, how is Geoffrey?"

"The same, my lady."

"You said you were concerned. Is he still speaking of revolution?"

"He has said nothing to me since the day of the fire. I think that he does not trust me."

"And do you trust him?" she asked.

He mulled it over. "I do not trust human nature," he said at last. "And I do not trust his nature."

"I see. I could not find him this morning."

"Oh, as to that, it is not suspicious," Stanley said. "He said he was to find a blacksmith to make repairs on our coach."

"Ah! Good."

* * *

Cordelia had one hand on the side of the gig, ready to cling on if they hit a particularly bad rut or pothole, but she had discovered the secret to a half-comfortable ride was to relax as much as possible. And Stanley was accomplished at steering the horse around the worst of the potential jolts. She wondered how the axle had broken on her travelling chariot. She could not have fallen asleep on the journey, but she let her eyes flutter closed and her brain to spin around the recent events.

Always, she was fighting her scatter-gun nature to veer off on interesting tangents. She knew it to be her greatest fault. She carried a notebook in her bag to jot down ideas as they came to her. She had found that if she did not, then the ideas would instead crowd around in her head and give her no rest. She would forget her previous motivations, and jump after some new shiny butterfly of interest.

I am to find Lizzie's killer, she reminded herself. *I promised Ruby that I would do so, and also, it seems to me to be wrong that no one else is particularly concerned about it.*

And perhaps it was Percy, or some other lover, she thought.

Though I am still not convinced that Iris spoke the truth when she mentioned other men. So if it is Percy, what then? It still needs to be investigated and he needs to be brought to justice.

There is the matter of Iris. She pondered that for a little while. *Perhaps it is linked,* she thought, *and therefore I need to look into it. Certainly she has secrets and I wish to uncover them. She is lying about something.*

I do this for justice. She smiled. *But I am also very nosey.*

And her nosiness led her, as soon as they arrived at Four Trees, to go back up to the room that Lizzie and Iris had shared.

She looked around. Lizzie's things had been tidied into her chest; she assumed that Iris had done it. Of Iris herself, no sign remained. She knelt down awkwardly and looked under Iris's bed, and under her thin mattress, but there was nothing.

She turned to the space that Lizzie had occupied. She sat on the bed and dragged the chest closer, flipping it open. On the inside of the lid were pasted images cut from magazines. There was a bucolic scene of a cottage and a river, and on the grassy bank a pair of lovers were entwined. He was dressed as a soldier, Cordelia noted. There were other images, cut and pasted in a decoupage style; a robin, some turtle-doves, a bunch of roses, all arranged around the edges of the lid. It was a common enough thing to do, when one carried one's whole home in a small wooden chest.

She dug deeper into the chest. She felt a little wrong, as if she was invading the girl's private property, but no one had come to claim it.

Had Maude really written to her family? Had she received word back? Cordelia resolved to ask.

There were two gowns in the chest, both fine but patched and of an older style made up to be more modern. There were a few copies of illustrated magazines for ladies, and the usual assortment of plain-worked undergarments. There was a pristine set of satin gloves, clearly put aside for some dream of attending a ball.

And there was, at last, a small and thick letter tied up with a thin and frayed ribbon.

Now this felt like the greatest violation of all. Cordelia drew the packet onto her lap and held it for a moment, questioning her own actions.

It had to be done. She picked apart the knot and looked at the letter, feeling the good-quality thick paper, all folded up small.

She opened it out and saw that the writer of the letter had left large margins around the edges, and wrote with a heavy hand, pressing grooves into the paper. They had a large and almost childish style of handwriting. And it was not dated.

She flicked straight to the end.

"P."

It was Percy, she was sure of it.

It was going to be a love letter, and she almost wanted to read it with her eyes closed. She blinked and forced herself to look. She couldn't help glancing up at the door, as if she thought Lizzie was going to walk in and discover her most private correspondence being violated.

Oh, that she would walk in.

Cordelia reminded herself why she was doing this, and read the short missive.

"Lizzie,

I admire you very much and you are a wonderful woman and I am sure you will make a good wife for an honest man.

But I am not that man.

The fault is with me, not with you. If I gave you any sign then I am sorry for it.

Do not think of me. Let me be dead to you. I am a soldier. I will always leave. Always.

Yours in affection,

P."

Cordelia read it once more, but it seemed to be a plain and honest message: *leave me alone.* There was no code or hidden meaning. Percy had been as direct as he could.

And love-struck Lizzie had kept the letter, tied up in string. If Cordelia had received such a letter, she would have burned it, and then would have wanted to paint her face with the ash and make a scene on the gentleman's front lawn.

She felt sorry for Percy, in a small way. This letter matched exactly with what he had told her in the inn; that she had been infatuated with him, but that they had not been lovers.

But you did give her some sign, she thought, her sympathy quickly fading. *You did say you walked out together; for many a young woman, that is sign enough. You are old enough to know far better than this.*

Iris had suggested that Lizzie had other men. There was no sign of it in the chest. She would not have kept the letter if she had moved on to another lover. Iris lied; why? Cordelia bent and riffled through the rest of the tawdry belongings, but no more letters were revealed.

She didn't seem like the type to dally in this way, Cordelia thought. *She was a poor girl from a once-rich family; she'd have standards. She would want marriage, above all.*

Goodness, why did the silly chit ever think she'd find security with a soldier? Then Cordelia remembered he was an officer and quite soon to be expected to retire on a nice pension.

Officers were gentlemen; they were generally respectable, depending on rank. Cordelia couldn't imagine Percy retiring. What would he do? It was hard to imagine him mingling with the other military men she'd met. There was an earthiness to him, a roughness she supposed he'd picked up on long campaigns. He wasn't a dinner-party-colonel, by any means.

Cordelia stood up and took the letter with her. It was evidence, she realised. Evidence against Percy Slatters.

Was it enough of a motive? He'd loved and left other women; she had seen that for her own eyes when that woman, Delilah, had come to the mill demanding reparation. Had he killed before, as well? Cordelia was growing cold in the room, and began to make her way back to the main rooms downstairs as she tried to imagine the dashing Captain seducing and murdering his way across the British Isles.

And still something nagged at her; some chance remark from the meeting in the inn. Something about the Battle of Waterloo.

CHAPTER FOURTEEN

"What do you know about Waterloo?" Cordelia said to Ruby, late that night as they prepared for their beds.

Ruby was sliding a warmed brick to the bottom of Cordelia's bed. She pulled the covers up tight, and patted them neatly into place. "Nothing, my lady. We kicked Boney's — ah, excuse me. We won, that's it, and huzzah for that."

"It was before either of us were born," Cordelia mused. "Something is on my mind. Well, I am sure it will come back to me." She stood by the fire. It had been well banked up with coals so that it would last the night in a smouldering state, and give off enough heat that they wouldn't wake to ice on the insides of the windows. That had happened twice in the past week, and Cordelia had decided that enough was enough. It wasn't common to heat a bedroom, particularly at night, but Cordelia had decided to be uncommon — and comfortable. Her aunt could afford the coal. She rolled the glass of warm mulled cider against her chest as she pondered the situation. "No word of Iris?"

"None. I asked for any information but no one could say where she came from. How on earth did your aunt engage her services?"

"She simply turned up, like that travelling quilt-maker did the past week. The quilter was sent away. But Iris was engaged to stay."

"With no recommendations?"

"I believe she had a letter with her." Cordelia sighed. "We need to talk to Lizzie's family. I wonder if my aunt wrote to them."

"Why? Lizzie had no contact with them. Not for a long time. Her parents were dead, I think, and her siblings married off. They saw her as an inconvenience that had to be got out of the way."

"They might know something — some reason she would be killed."

"I doubt it. I am starting to think it was a lover's tryst gone wrong."

Cordelia shook her head. "No, I don't see that. She only had eyes for Percy, and he did not want her at all."

"Then it was him!" Ruby said vehemently. "Percy."

Cordelia didn't answer. She looked past Ruby to the

window behind her. There was a gap in the curtain, and through it shone a strange white light. She was reminded of the red glow when the fire had started, and with a sick feeling she crossed the room quickly.

"Oh!" She peered through, and then swung the curtains open in delight. Her sick feeling turned to joy. "Look, Ruby! Snow! It is snowing at last!"

Ruby rolled her eyes dramatically. "You're no better than a child," she muttered, but she joined Cordelia at the window, a slight smile on her lips.

"Oh, come on. You must admit it looks magical. And so peaceful."

"That's because you can spend your time inside, by the fire. For those who are out in it, or who have no fire lit, or whose journeys are delayed or work postponed…"

Cordelia elbowed Ruby in the ribs. "Hush, you misery-maker. Put your political speech aside. Let us enjoy it." She rubbed at the glass, smearing away the condensation. "Ruby, look. Do you see a figure out there?" Immediately, her sick feeling returned as all the events of the past few weeks coalesced. Murder and riots and incendiarism — this was a dangerous place to be, in truth.

Ruby pressed close to the glass. "My lady," she said in a low whisper. "It is a man with a gun."

* * *

Cordelia allowed herself about twenty seconds of internal screaming panic. She downed the tepid remains of her cider and made a decision.

"Stay here, Ruby. Watch that figure. I want to know what they do and where they go. I am going to rouse Geoffrey and Stanley."

"You would send them out after an armed man?"

"You're right. Not poor Stanley. I should only send Geoffrey."

"No, I mean—"

Cordelia smiled. "What do *you* think he keeps in the sword case on the back of the carriage? Pork pies?"

With that, she left Ruby and ran down to the stables area. She was dressed for bed, in light slippers and a long nightdress and housecoat, her hair lightly twisted up in a turban. She didn't care; she was sure Geoffrey would have seen all manner of sights in his time, and as for Stanley … well, the lad would recover soon enough from the shock of seeing her in disarray.

She paused at the back door of the kitchen. Outside, the snow was swirling in light eddies, but the ground was already covered. "Ah, dash it all," she muttered, and jumped out into the cold. Her feet sank into the white stuff and were instantly struck by a bone-bitingly freezing sensation. She ran and reached the door of the shared room, and hammered on it frantically.

"Wake up!"

The door opened and Geoffrey stood there, still dressed though a little dishevelled, and he gaped in horror. "My lady!"

"There is someone at the front of the house carrying a gun," she said. She didn't need to explain anything else. He snapped straight to attention.

"Stanley," he growled over his shoulder, "get out of bed, and let's see what sort of man you can be. My lady, you get back into the house and bolt everything. Get all of you in one room, the strongest room there is. And I ... will see to this. Now, move, all of you!"

He ordered, and she obeyed, grateful and relieved to be able to hand the responsibility for part of the situation over to someone else. She still had her own duties, and she took them up immediately. "I left Ruby watching out of the bedroom window," she informed him. "I'll return to her and find out where the gunman is, and come back to you with the information."

He blinked, and then snorted. "My lady, it is snowing."

"Yes, I—"

"So there will be footprints. Now get you all to safety."

She knew that she blushed at her own idiocy, and she turned away while Geoffrey went deeper in the shadows of the room. She ran lightly across the courtyard back to the kitchen, and when she looked back, Geoffrey was a black silhouette in the snow flurries, holding a long rifle. He was doing something to the end, and she realised, as he held it aloft, that he was fixing a bayonet to the muzzle.

She hoped the snow would still be white in the morning.

With that dreadful image in her head, she ran back up the stairs to fetch Ruby.

"Where is the figure now?"

"Still there — they walked to one side of the lawns and stopped and now they've just walked back to where they started."

"I've sent Geoffrey out there. He is armed. We are to get Maude and Kate and the cook, and all of us hide in a room."

"Goodness," Ruby said, trying to make light of the situation as she followed Cordelia out of their shared room. "This is a new thing for you, surely. I can scarce believe it. Have you ever hidden from anything ever before?"

Cordelia stopped walking. "Yes," she said thickly. "Him."

"Who?"

"My late husband was … sometimes in an ill humour. Thank God you never met him. Now, let us wake Maude;

I will go in, but you stay in the corridor. I do not imagine she is going to react well."

Cordelia knocked on Maude's door but she did so for propriety's sake; she did not expect a reply, nor did she receive one. She took a deep breath and pushed the heavy oak door open.

"Maude ... Maude!" she said in the sort of loud whisper that people only used at night when they wanted to wake someone up without actually seeming like they were waking them up. It would have made more sense to speak normally. She coughed and said, "Maude, wake up!"

The curtains in Maude's room were open, and the place was icy-cold. By the ethereal light of the moon on snow, the room was lit enough to see well within.

And Cordelia saw that Maude was not there.

She rushed in with a cry, as if somehow her aunt might be hiding behind a pillow, but the bed and the whole room was thoroughly unoccupied. Ruby followed, alerted by her shout.

"She's not here!" Cordelia said in panic.

"Let us check the other rooms," Ruby said. "Maybe she is one of those who creep to the kitchen at night, to secretly eat cheese."

"You are right—"

And then a gunshot tore through the silent air.

* * *

Against all good sense, they both ran towards the sound of the shot. Cook emerged from her room and from another doorway came Kate, rubbing her eyes and throwing a shawl around her shoulders. Cordelia ordered them all to gather in the servants' hall while she herself ignored their protests and ran to the front door, wrenching it open. Her feet were soaked through and she could barely feel anything below the ankles now. It was an old manor house, lacking the porch and pillars of newer places, and as soon as she left the house she realised how exposed she was.

Her heart was hammering as she looked through the swirling snowflakes, trying to see what was happening. Only her feet were cold; the rest of her was warmed by fear and tension.

There was a dark shape approaching.

No, two dark shapes.

Two figures, and one carried two guns, while the other, the shorter person, staggered and stumbled.

"Geoffrey…" Cordelia called. Ruby appeared at Cordelia's back, then, and passed her mistress something heavy and long and cold to the touch.

"Take this poker, my lady, and aim for anywhere soft."

"And you?"

"I have a meat cleaver, don't worry."

"Right."

An eddy of snow cut the figures off for a moment, but as quickly as the white storm came down, it swirled away again, and now she could see both of them clearly.

She dropped the poker with a clang, and ran down the steps.

"Geoffrey! And oh my goodness, Maude, dear aunt, what on earth … there is an armed man abroad, and you must not…"

"There is but one armed man out here tonight, my lady, and it is I," Geoffrey said, in a bored tone, as if he apprehended villains on a nightly basis.

Maude looked down and her shamefaced air told Cordelia who she had seen from the window. It had been Maude. She glanced at the two weapons tucked under Geoffrey's right arm. "Aunt? It was you? You were out … with a gun?"

"Let's get madam inside," Geoffrey said, and Maude did not fight it when he took one side and Cordelia the other. By the time they got to her bedroom, by slow and painful steps, Ruby and Kate had already warmed her bed and brought a glass of wine.

Maude was put to bed without a murmur.

* * *

Cordelia barely slept that night, and she felt like death

warmed over at breakfast the next morning.

Maude, likewise, did not look terribly perky.

The pair of them sat in a foggy-headed silence until their strong cups of tea began to filter through their systems. Maude ploughed through three slices of plain toast before finally speaking.

"I've not been sleeping well, you know."

What a revelation, Cordelia thought. "I am sorry to hear that. Um…"

"And you want to know why I was outside with a shotgun."

Cordelia mostly wanted to know *how* she had been outside with a shotgun. The frail older lady sometimes struggled to lift a particularly heavy piece of cake to her mouth. Guns were not light objects. But she nodded, and said, "I would like to know, yes."

Maude waved her wrinkled hand and Kate darted forward to refill her cup. "I wake at every noise," she said. "I toss and I turn and I imagine all manner of dire deeds occurring. I run hot and cold, hot and cold, and sometimes I itch all over. Last night, I was sure that someone was out there."

"So you took up a gun and went out?" Cordelia shook her head in exasperation. "My dear aunt. You should have woken me, or one of the servants."

"Well, I did, in the end, did I not?" Maude would not meet Cordelia's eyes and she realised that her aunt was actually a little embarrassed about the whole affair. "It is strange how things — decisions — at night seem to make a lot of sense but when you look at them again in the daytime, you realise what a silly old fool you've been."

"Oh, Maude. I wonder if we might send for the doctor? Have you always struggled to sleep?"

"It is only since the murder that I have had these problems," Maude said. "I slept like a babe before then. Nothing would wake me! And now everything is turned upside down. Oh, there is no reason to send for the doctor. Things will settle down soon, I am sure."

* * *

Cordelia was not so sure. She said as much to Ruby a little later. Ruby fussed with Cordelia's hair and prepared her for the upcoming trip to church.

"I don't like the sound of my aunt's health at the moment," she said. "She is not young but oh! I wish she were not so stubborn. I really do not want to leave her here alone. Especially not in this state."

"I know," Ruby said, misting some spray onto the ringlets she had created around Cordelia's ears. "It is a strange change in her indeed."

"It is understandable, of course, if she imagines a

169

murderer to be roaming around."

Ruby put the glass bottle and its tubing down and looked at Cordelia in the mirror. "I think there is more to it than that," she said. "I would look deeper. My lady, may I be excused the service this morning? There is mending to be done."

"Really? We have had such long empty hours here that I can't imagine there's a single scrap of my clothing that has escaped your needle."

"There is always more to do."

"Go on with you." Cordelia smiled. "I am sure you will spend the morning in profitable contemplation." She stood up and gathered up her outdoor things. "And not in reading that terrible novel I saw on your bed earlier…"

"My lady, of course not. On a Sunday!"

"Don't worry. The ravishing hero turns out to be a vicar. So it's probably all right to read on the Sabbath."

Cordelia was half out of the door before Ruby spluttered, "What, wait, so you've read it?"

Chapter Fifteen

The antics of Saturday night had left Cordelia with a dull headache and Sunday morning's interminable sermon did not improve matters. She felt lacklustre and ill at ease on Monday, and sat to compose some letters home, instructing her staff to begin preparations for Christmas. She intended to celebrate quietly at home. She had received a number of invitations which she had declined, all but a New Year's Eve ball. That sounded fun.

So there was not a great deal of preparation that needed to be done, in truth, but still she chafed, feeling caught between two forces.

But her house would still be there — she felt a thrill of triumph again at that thought — and her greater need was here. *Needs,* she corrected herself. The matter of the murder *and* the matter of her aunt.

She sat at a small corner table in the sitting room while

Maude settled into her armchair by the fire, and dozed. She was just composing a list of foods that she wanted to be prepared on Christmas Day when there was a sharp rap on the door and Ruby burst in.

Maude was instantly awake, and somewhat sniffy at the young woman's intrusion. She did not seem ready to ever accept Ruby as a real lady's maid. But she said nothing, and simply glowered from the depths of her chair.

Ruby made a shallow bob towards Maude as she began babbling in a rush to Cordelia. "My lady, I have been in town with Stanley, as you directed. You must come!"

"What are you doing sending that chit to town?" Maude asked, leaning forward.

Cordelia coughed. "I, er, she was purchasing some ribbon—"

"Oh yes, exactly that," Ruby agreed. "Yes, some lovely tartan stuff. But my lady, it is Iris — she has been found."

Cordelia packed up her portable writing desk, smudging the undried ink on at least two letters, and followed Ruby quickly from the room.

* * *

Ruby told her that Stanley was waiting outside in the gig. Cordelia ran up to her room, grabbed her cloak and hat and gloves, and as she ran back down, Ruby explained what had transpired.

172

"We went to find Percy as you directed, my lady, but as we went to the garrison there was something happening. Stanley, that wet lad, said I didn't ought to have carried on, but he hides from bees and spiders, so I ignored him. Anyway Iris was just outside the garrison, all muffled up in scarves, and they were surrounding her and arresting her! So we knew you would want to come and see. I can't believe she didn't flee this place completely!"

"You did well." Cordelia stopped and sighed in exasperation as soon as she reached the gig. Her chariot was clearly still unavailable, and she did not want to take her aunt's carriage without permission; permission she was unlikely to get. "Ah, bother. This is a two-person vehicle."

"Stanley doesn't really count as a full person," Ruby said. "Budge up, you skinny sot."

It was a very tight squeeze, but at least they all stayed warm, even if Stanley had to lean forward to give him the elbow-room to haul on the reins. He was forced to poke out into the rain, but he claimed not to mind. Ruby muttered something about him enjoying suffering because it was for the sake of his soul.

Still, Cordelia was grateful when they reached the town and she popped like a cork from a bottle to land on her feet on the ice-hard ground. It had stopped snowing early in the morning, and though the hills were blanketed with fresh, crisp whiteness, already the tracks and roads were black and grey once more. "Do you know where they took her?" Cordelia asked Ruby who remained up on the gig's bench seat. "Is there a lock-up in this town? Oh, ugh. Don't tell me I have to seek out that odious constable."

"I don't know about a lock-up," Ruby said, "but they were saying they would take her to the inn."

"Of course." Cordelia looked up at the steps of the warm and welcoming place. "Stanley…"

"It's all right, my lady, I won't freeze to death. One of us does need to stay with the horse."

"Go around to the inn's yard and find a fire, at least," she instructed. "Ruby, will you go back to the garrison and find out why Iris was there, what she did, who she spoke to and everything else that you can discover."

"And you get to go into a nice warm inn," Ruby said petulantly.

"And you get to look at nice warm soldiers, so don't complain," Cordelia replied. "I am sure you can rub two of them together to make a fire. Now, go."

This time, when Cordelia entered the inn, she didn't try to evade the maid who lurked in the hallway. Instead she made a beeline for her.

"Good morning. I am looking for Iris Fletcher."

"You and half the town, I hear," a man chortled,

standing off to one side. She turned her glare at him. He was holding a thick pad of paper and a pencil. "What is your involvement here?" he asked.

"I beg your pardon," she replied, in full-on *I Am A Lady* mode. She ratcheted up her accent a few notches. She could cut glass with the enunciation of her consonants. "What is *your* involvement?"

"I'm from the Gazette. Shocking business, ain't it? A right rum do."

She looked him up and down. "Yes. The newspaper trade is, indeed, a shocking business. Stirring up panic with lies and rumour…"

"No, I meant—"

"I think not."

"Eh?"

Cordelia turned back to the maid. "Is this man bothering you?"

The maid was wide-eyed. "I have asked him to leave but he says he won't go till he gets to talk to that girl what we have here, that Ms Fletcher."

The newspaper man had a crooked smile but it drooped as she advanced upon him. She was pleased to find she was an inch or so taller than him, and probably as wide. He didn't look like he spent much time in any physical activity. She tipped her chin up and regarded him with the most supercilious air she could muster. She stepped forward into his personal space, and he reacted automatically, stumbling backwards.

She had the advantage and she pressed on, speaking as she did so.

"I would ask, *don't you know who I am*, but it is clearly pointless, because if you *knew* who I am and who my husband is, you would not still be standing there like that, but instead, you would be scurrying backwards and grovelling for forgiveness even as you tried to escape *before* my lord arrives as he is expected to do in just *one minute* and you had better hope that he has brought only his sword stick and not his — oh, you're leaving, so soon before making his acquaintance?"

"Madam, forgive me, but urgent business…"

She smiled, and let him scurry away. He was frowning, but he looked around like a rat exploring a kitchen.

"My lady," the maid whispered, bobbing up and down furiously.

"Ah, yes. Now, where were we? You were to show me to Miss Fletcher, I believe."

"No, I…" The maid caught Cordelia's eye very briefly and immediately lowered her gaze. "Yes, my lady. Directly. Ah, your husband…?"

"If he does turn up, he will want to head straight for

the bar. He has not had a drink for many years, mostly on account of being dead."

The maid bit her lip and gave up trying to formulate any response to that. "This way, my lady."

Cordelia followed the maid through some grand double doors at the rear of the entrance lobby. The corridor led past some private rooms but quickly lost its shine and glamour as it became a service area for staff rather than anything for public view. Now they walked on bare stairs that rose up, narrowly, to a dark corridor on the first floor.

"Are these rooms vacant?" Cordelia asked.

"These are where servants stay when they are here with their households at the inn," the maid said. "But we get precious few such travellers now the roads are better, and people can push on through to Harrogate or York."

At the sound of their voices, a door halfway down the passageway opened, and Constable Kennett poked his head out. He looked surprised to see Cordelia, but he was quick to seize the opportunity.

Her heart sank.

He came out fully and waved his hand brusquely at the maid. "Get you back to work, such as it is, whatever work you actually do," he said. "I am far better served to deal with Lady Cornbrook than you are."

The maid darted away. Cordelia stifled her sigh, and

smiled very thinly. "Mr Kennett," she said. "I wonder if I might be allowed a brief moment to speak with the poor Miss Fletcher."

"Why? I mean, forgive me for asking and so on, but I don't rightly see as it is your place. Begging your pardon et cetera."

She tried to look pious, but was not sure exactly how, except by folding her hands together in front and pinching in her cheeks a little. "As a good Christian woman it is my duty to follow the example of *our* saviour and attend to the most vulnerable in our society, our community, and indeed, I feel *called* to bring what little relief I can to this poor, dear girl in her hour of greatest need."

"This murderer," he said.

"It is not for me to judge."

"It is not. You are right, there." He began to advance upon her. His face was shiny and the skin was pink, and seemed as if it were stretched or inflated over his face. He had scabs at the corner of his mouth, and his greasy dark brown coat released a stale odour as he raised his left arm to lean against the wall. In a young, lithe man, the attitude would have been compelling. She could imagine John Kitt standing like that, with the air of a pugilist awaiting a bout in the ring. But Kennett's affectation made him look like a clumsy actor. "Now, Lady C, if I might be so bold—"

"Cornbrook," she interrupted swiftly.

"Quite so, yes," he said, with clearly no intention of paying her the correct courtesy. "Lady C, here you are, and here I am, and might I say, what an uncommon situation this is, indeed, so it is."

He was a self-taught man, she saw in a flash. His verbosity came from reading and absorbing and trying to sound far more intelligent than he was. She knew he was susceptible to flattery, but she wondered how much ale he had imbibed, and how that affected him. In her late husband, it had stirred mindless violence but she had seen others taken by alcohol in different ways. Without knowing his reactions, she was reluctant to push him.

She took a step back to get out of the range of his rank breath, but he pushed himself away from the wall and moved around her, forcing her to suddenly turn so that she faced the way she had come.

The way which was now blocked by Kennett.

He smiled. "But perhaps, Lady C, I am in a position to help you. After all, you are here because you want something. Now, is it not the way of the world that one good deed does deserve another, as they say, if you like?"

There was nothing now on his face except the smug triumph of a lecherous man who had trapped his quarry.

He stepped forward and now it was her turn to step

back, just as she had forced the newspaper man to do earlier. Her back was against the wall. She was wearing too many skirts to kick out at him, but perhaps she could make use of a hatpin as she had done in the past.

She began to inch her hand up, as if to casually pat her hair. But he caught it, gripping her wrist in his sweaty palm, his fingers tight around her. "Oh, no, Lady C," he said, dropping his voice low. "I do not think you shall—"

"Actually, *I* do not think you shall!" said a new voice from behind him.

Smack.

Kennett's eyes rolled to the side and then upwards as his jaw went slack. He staggered sideways, his shoulder colliding with the wall, and as he moved, Ruby was revealed to be standing behind him.

She had a heavy wooden implement held in both her hands, and wide grin on her face.

"Is that a barometer?" Cordelia said.

"Why, yes, it is, my lady."

"Oh. Jolly good."

Kennett snuffled and bent over, breathing heavily and muttering.

"He's still alive," Ruby said jovially. "Shall I hit him again, my lady?"

CHAPTER SIXTEEN

"No," both Kennett and Cordelia said at once. Kennett raised one hand unsteadily.

"No," he repeated. "I don't know ... what ... who is that? Why..."

"He's not dead but I suspect he's lightly concussed," Cordelia said. "Here, constable, sit down before you fall down."

He folded up and slithered down the wall until he was sitting on the floor, his eyes fluttering open and closed. "Ruby, stay with him. If he falls asleep, wake him up."

"I would prefer him to sleep."

"Trust me," Cordelia said. "If he sleeps when he is injured he may not wake."

"Let me sleep," he whispered.

Ruby hefted the barometer in her hands. "Sorry, sir," she said cheerily. "You heard my lady. I can't let you do that."

Cordelia left them to it. She approached the door that Kennett had appeared from, and pushed it open warily. She found herself immediately in a small anteroom, only a few feet square, with another door leading from it. That door was closed, and there was a large, solid key in the lock.

She turned the key, but also knocked as she pushed the door open, saying, "Miss Fletcher? It is I, Lady Cornbrook. Do not be alarmed." She meant, of course, *do not think it's the constable again, and try to spring upon me to effect a dramatic escape.*

The room was larger than Cordelia had expected, and Iris was sitting on the bed at the far end, by a window with small black leads running in diagonals to create a diamond pattern of glass. Even if she threw the chair through the window to smash it, she would have to fight the soft metal and it wouldn't be a quick or easy way to flee.

She looked up at Cordelia, and looked down again instantly. She was sitting all tightly drawn in on herself, her legs together and her hands in her lap, and her shoulders bent and rounded. She was dressed in a plain brown dress, of a modern style with wide skirts, but neatly and unfussily sewn and made, with no extraneous lace or frippery. She wore a bonnet on her head, and looked every inch the demure maid — and not at all like she had presented herself at the mill. *She does not tell the truth*, Cordelia reminded herself.

"Are they keeping you well?" Cordelia said, pulling the door closed behind her.

Iris waved a hand to the table. "Well enough, my lady," she whispered. There was a jug of water, a plate with half a bread roll, and a Bible placed there. "I have the essentials."

"Except your freedom." Cordelia walked over and sat on the far end of the bed, keeping a respectful distance between them. She watched Iris carefully. The young woman was pale, and swallowing nervously. "On what grounds are they keeping you here? Have they told you?"

She flared her nostrils as she dragged in a heavy breath. "In one moment they are saying it is because I left my situation at Miss Stanbury's, but that is wrong, for I was not in any situation there. They say I stole things, but I took nothing. And then in the next moment they say I am to be investigated for the murder of Lizzie and that is … that is … oh, my lady, what shall I do?"

"You can only tell the truth, girl," Cordelia said, firmly. "I know you have a deep faith and you must trust in that. Be honest." She wondered how Iris measured her truthfulness. Her faith seemed very sincere. Perhaps it trumped all other things.

"But my honesty … is worth nothing. Who will believe me? I would be better with a good lie," Iris said, and there was unmistakeable bitterness in her voice. It surprised Cordelia. The seamstress was all meek and mild on the outside, but there were strange currents flowing through her.

"Where do you come from, Iris? Perhaps I can get word to your family. You must have distant relatives, cousins, perhaps."

Iris huffed, an inelegant sound. "That I do doubt. I never did find any of them again."

"I beg your pardon?"

Iris picked at a seam on her skirts, pushing at it with her thumbnail. After a short silence, she seemed to decide she would talk, and talk she did. "Well, my lady, my family's all gone, you see. I left home when I was twelve to apprentice to my aunt and she lived in a city and all was good. But after five years, my aunt died, and I had nothing then; her family which did ought to have been considered my family threw me out so I went home. And home? Home was nothing. Empty and no word of where they might have gone."

"What, did the neighbours not tell you anything?"

Iris shook her head. "No neighbours left neither. The whole village was gone, just about, to the mills in the towns I think. All gone."

"And so you became a travelling seamstress."

"Indeed, my lady. I thought I could not fall lower but here I am."

"And quite friendless also," Cordelia said, half to herself.

Iris fell silent again.

"Iris, this is a bad position you are in. You shared a room with Lizzie, and you told me she had no lovers, but then you changed this and told me that she did. You alluded to many of them, in fact. Is this truly the case? Tell me the truth this time."

Iris chewed her lip briefly. She nodded, then shook her head, as if listening to a far-away voice. "My lady, it would be wrong of me to speak ill of the dead." Suddenly she looked up and met Cordelia's gaze. Her eyes were large and shining. "For the dead are all around us, do you know that? Can you feel them as I feel them?"

Cordelia wanted to edge away. A crackle of that strange energy she had felt before, when Iris had come to the mill, fizzed in the air. Cordelia held her position and said, "I fear that I do not. It must be a remarkable gift that you have. But would Lizzie not want you to speak the truth, after all, so that her death might be avenged?"

"Yes. No. I don't know. I don't know the truth. Do any of us? For now we see through a glass, darkly…"

Oh, infuriating girl. Cordelia said, "Just tell me. Did she have a lover? One lover only? Wasn't Percy Slatters her lover?"

"In her head, my lady, perhaps he was. She wanted it but I would say that she wanted anyone, anyone who would marry her. That is how it was."

"I see. And was there anyone else that she walked out with?"

"I know not … no, my lady. There was no one else. Better had it been for her if there had have been someone else, my lady. Anyone but him."

"And was she in the habit of meeting him, or anyone, not necessarily a lover, at the Ally Cross?"

"Who?"

"John Kitt? For he gave her his pamphlet to read … and you, also."

"She reported him, my lady, to the authorities. She would not listen to him."

Ah! That was as Kennett had said — Kitt had been in trouble before, and it must have been her, if not others as well. "So she was not regularly meeting Kitt? In fact, she thwarted or spurned him?"

Iris began to rock to and fro, a tiny but telling movement. Now, her hands were clutching her skirts. With an effort, she said, "Yes, my lady. And … there is more I must tell you."

186

Cordelia waited.

"She … I am so sorry, my lady, but she was drugging your aunt!"

That was the last thing Cordelia expected to hear. Iris was staring down again, and Cordelia frowned. "She was doing what?"

"She was giving Miss Stanbury laudanum to help her to sleep, so that she would not wake up when Lizzie went off at night."

"Goodness." *Lizzie must have been seeing more of Percy than he admitted to.* "How do you know this for certain?"

"We shared a room, and I saw her, and I asked her what she was doing, and she said I must not tell, or she would accuse me of stealing and have me arrested. She said that she would put items in my chest and say I had taken them."

"And so you did not tell Miss Stanbury about this, or anyone else?"

"No, my lady. I am sorry. But it did her no harm — your aunt, I mean."

It would explain Maude's problems currently with sleeping, Cordelia realised. *She's no longer being drugged on a nightly basis.* "I am sorry you had to hold that secret. It must have been difficult."

Iris risked a tiny smile, flitting across her face. "Thank

you, my lady. I had no one to turn to."

"And is there anything else you can tell me about Lizzie? Anything at all, however small?"

"No, my lady. I am sorry. Except that—"

"Go on."

"Well, except that, why would I kill her? They say I might be the murderer. But why would I do that?"

"Why indeed," Cordelia said. She stood up and adjusted her petticoats. "Thank you for speaking so frankly to me, Miss Fletcher. Please try not to worry. One last thing. Is that constable bothering you? I know he has a way about him…"

There was a scornful tone in Iris's reply. "He's hardly the worst I've ever dealt with."

Again, Cordelia thought, *she's not so shy as she might seem.* "Good day, Miss Fletcher. All will be well."

CHAPTER SEVENTEEN

Constable Kennett was back on his feet when she emerged into the corridor, and Ruby was standing a few feet away, gripping the barometer with deadly intent. Cordelia nodded slightly at the glowering constable, and took Ruby's arm to lead her away.

"Wait up," he called. "Hold your horses, there, Lady C. Did you discover anything of import and so on?"

She ignored him and they descended the stairs. After a quick conversation with the maid in the entrance hall, they ensconced themselves in a private room and ordered a light midday meal, over which Cordelia sketched out what she'd learned from Iris.

"This is a mess," Ruby said at the end. "I suppose the letter, and what Percy says, and what Iris says does all match up at least; Lizzie had a candle for him but it was unrequited."

"That still makes him a suspect. And they *were* meeting,

at least for a while."

"Indeed it does, my lady. But do you believe Iris that Lizzie only met Percy? She has changed her story more than once."

"I do because Lizzie will have wanted marriage. And he is an officer."

Ruby pondered it. "You know, he is an old man, really. Perhaps she hoped that he might soon die. I wonder how desperate she was for marriage and security?"

"She gave out that she had standards. She was gently bred."

"She was poor," Ruby pointed out. "And standards mean nothing when you want a home and food and children."

"Indeed. Yet I cannot see her setting her sights on anyone of too low a birth."

Ruby shrugged. "As to that, perhaps she was practising her wiles on them."

"You cannot be serious!"

"Maybe," Ruby said. "We are not born coquettes. Why, as to myself, I have honed my skills over many years. I used to—"

"Stop there, thank you," Cordelia advised. "Now, will you go down to fetch more wine, please? And a cake of some sort. I am heartily sick of my aunt's plain fare and watered drinks."

"Willingly."

Ruby skipped off, and Cordelia sat back on the plush padded chair, steepling her hands and half-closing her eyes. *I believe Iris, at least in this matter; Lizzie and Percy walked out, frequently. He tired of her. And now he denies there was much to their relationship as he is afraid of suspicion falling on him... And she longed for him. Percy is a suspect,* she thought. *But so is Iris.*

For in spite of Cordelia's assurances to the young seamstress, she harboured suspicions about the woman. She was too layered, like an onion. One would peel back the shyness and find religious zealotry and underneath that, another layer, this one of superstition and folklore, and underneath *that* — who knew what lay beneath?

She must have dozed off, because she suddenly came to with a start. Her mouth was dry. Had she been sleeping and snoring? For a moment, Cordelia was confused, and wondered if she had been drugged herself.

But no. She was still in the inn, and she was held upright by her solid corsetry and the wide curving wooden arms of the chair. She reached out to take a sip of drink but it was empty, and she remembered that she had sent Ruby to fetch more. She had no idea how much time had passed. She could have slept for a moment, or an hour.

Still, it was odd that her maid had not yet returned.

She gathered up her things. She checked that her purse was still on her person, with her notebook and comb and pins and handkerchief and spare ribbon and keys and all the other clutter that seemed to live in her bag. She poked her head out into the corridor, but it was empty. Laughter and chatter drifted up from the bars and public rooms at the far end. Lunchtime trade, she surmised. And those who came to drink all afternoon, too.

She headed to the entrance hall. It was empty, the maid clearly called away on other business. She glanced at the door to the respectable saloon bar, but not much noise issued through it. Feeling daring, she put her hand to the door of the public bar, and peered in.

Inside, it was almost foetid in its warmth and dampness. There were mostly men within, but enough of a smattering of women to make it feel lively rather than intimidating. Heads turned as she entered, however. Everything about Cordelia — her clothing and her hair, her way of walking even before she opened her mouth — screamed "quality" and she was decidedly out of place.

But one's elevated rank was an armour, of sorts. She gazed around, looking for Ruby. She saw her, but at the same instant she saw who her maid was with.

Ah, she thought. *Captain Percy Slatters. Well done, Ruby. Find out as much as you can.*

She was about to retire, leaving her maid to ply whatever wiles she had, when Percy caught sight of her. His face creased in shock to see her in the bar, and he jumped to his feet, sweeping into a low bow.

"My dear lady," he said, coming forward with a startled urgency on his face. "Have you perhaps taken a wrong turn? It is rather busy here; please do allow me the courtesy of escorting you to a place more befitting."

She glanced past to see Ruby was fixing her with a fierce stare. Ruby then flicked her eyes towards the door, but shook her head slightly.

"Allow me one moment to talk with my maid," Cordelia said, and retreated out of the busy bar. Ruby followed.

As soon as they were in the quieter lobby, Ruby said, "I am sorry I took so long, my lady. I haven't even got the wine yet. But I'll join you presently back in the room, if you would care to go on up without me."

"What of Slatters?"

"Indeed," Ruby said. "Wait for me, and I shall tell all, my lady."

Cordelia felt rather as if she had been dismissed by her own lady's maid but she returned to the private room, and found that the dirty crockery had been cleared away. She sat, and within ten minutes, Ruby entered, bringing the long-awaited cake and a sweet wine.

"I have news to impart," Ruby said, her face wreathed in smiles.

Cordelia poured her a very small glass of wine. "Go on."

"It is about Percy and his lover," Ruby said.

"Lizzie? We know that already."

"Oh no, my lady," Ruby said, her smile now a broad and indecorous grin. "He's here to see his *current* lover. Iris Fletcher."

Cordelia hesitated. She stopped, stared, and then picked up the bottle of wine. "Here," she said. "Let me top up your glass…"

CHAPTER EIGHTEEN

It was a strange revelation to get one's head around, Cordelia thought. *And yet ... obvious now?* She mulled the new relationship over on their journey back to Four Trees that afternoon, and remained the rest of the day in Maude's sitting room, puzzling over it.

But Iris was a woman of layers, she reminded herself. *And here was a new thing indeed.* It confirmed Cordelia's suspicions that Iris was to be considered as a suspect in the case. For if Lizzie loved Percy but Percy loved Iris then that was a motive as large as any other. And it explained, perhaps, Iris's inconsistencies when speaking about Lizzie's relationship with Percy.

But there were problems with that scenario. Cordelia pulled a blanket around her shoulders and stared into the fire, trying to play it out in her head. *If Iris had killed Lizzie, why would Iris stay here at Four Trees? Just to be close to Percy?*

That was the biggest issue, and it kept Cordelia awake for most of Monday night. She started to consider laudanum for herself.

Tuesday dawned as a grey and unremarkable day. It was the sort of day that nothing happened on. No one remembered Tuesdays like this.

It became, however, a pivotal and historical day.

It was just after lunch when the word came. Cordelia had sent Kate to fetch Geoffrey so she could ask about the progress on the travelling chariot's repairs, but Kate did not return for half an hour. When she came back into the house, she was breathless and wide-eyed.

She was closely followed by Stanley who was stammering badly in his panic. The expressions on both servants stilled Maude's usually complaining tongue. She hissed, but let them speak.

"There is a riot, my lady, madam," Kate said, looking frantically from Maude to Cordelia and then to Stanley. "We have had word."

"Where is Geoffrey?" Cordelia demanded.

Stanley could barely get his words out. "I don't know," he eventually managed to say, and flushed scarlet.

"Not the mill again," Maude said. Her voice was high and wavery, and she looked more like the old woman that she truly was, than Cordelia had ever seen her.

Both Stanley and Kate nodded. Kate said, "Madam, they are said to have left the town and are making for the mill. They are calling upon the workers to smash the machines."

Maude gasped and deflated, emitting a sad little squeak as she sank back into her armchair. Kate took a step forward, and then stopped. Cordelia nodded her on, and Kate mustered her courage to attend to the stricken Maude. It was a measure of how upset Maude was that she let the maid of all work pat a blanket around her knees and offer her a comforting drink.

Cordelia straightened up. "Stanley, fetch Miss Stanbury's shotgun."

"My lady, I hardly think that she can—"

"Not for her, you daft brush. For you, to defend the house if you need to."

Stanley inflated his narrow chest and strode away like she'd just pinned a medal to him.

Ruby said, "And us?"

"Well, we don't have your preferred weapon to hand," Cordelia said. "I don't think there is a barometer in the house. In lieu of that, I intend to go out and find this damned coachman of mine."

"Geoffrey?"

"Indeed, the same. He has few uses, but protection is

one of them. And just when we need him, where is he?"

"My lady ... it is likely that we will find him with the rioters. He is becoming ..."

"Yes. Yes, he is, and I am going to put a stop to this," Cordelia said firmly.

"The riot?"

"Geoffrey's part in it, certainly. And the riot itself? Well, we shall see. I am mightily peeved, I can tell you that."

Ruby could make no reply to that. Together, they sallied forth, leaving the defence of Four Trees in the trembling hands of Stanley.

* * *

"This is a ridiculous idea, my lady," Ruby said as she jogged alongside Cordelia. Ruby was huffing and out of breath. Cordelia herself had a slight stitch in her side but she was not going to reveal that titbit of weakness.

"It is," Cordelia agreed. "Still, life is short, is it not? I've done ridiculous things nearly all my life and you know what? I'm still going forward. I may have fewer invitations to society balls, and no doubt I enliven many a parlour with salacious gossip, but it doesn't matter. Does it?"

"It depends on your priorities," Ruby muttered. "I suspect that I am utterly ruined for being in anyone else's service now; that is, if anyone would have me."

"Are you thinking of leaving me?"

"Well, no. But I'm just saying that your actions have a wider effect than you might think. *My lady.*"

Cordelia ignored the tone in Ruby's voice. They slowed their pace as they reached Simeon's house. Beyond, there lay the mill. "You said they were coming from the town to the mill?" Cordelia asked.

"Indeed so, my lady. Can you hear anything?"

"I am not sure. But I don't want to be trapped on this road. Look, up on the hill above. I think we ought to follow that path and get up there."

"I don't think it's a path," Ruby said. She followed Cordelia anyway.

In truth, it was more of a trail left by the small, hardy sheep that dotted the hillsides and moors. It was enough, however, to raise them above the scene at the mill.

And what a scene it was.

There was a seething throng of brown and beige and black and yellow and cream. The men and women of the town made a rippling mass as they surged around the mill. Hands were upraised in the air, clutching sticks and canes and any wooden implement they could find.

But no barometers, Cordelia marked. And more significantly, no edged weapons of any kind. The people might be protesting, but they seemed to intend to do it peacefully — relatively speaking. The common masses didn't own swords and the like, but nor had they come out with billhooks and poles. She expected scythes, too, but didn't see any. Maybe the sheep did all the work of keeping things cropped, or maybe not enough grew to warrant chopping down.

The ones at the front of the crowd were mostly young men. They shouted loudly, and she could see that their expressions were angry. They pressed forwards, calling out as they approached the main mill gates.

Behind them came more men, and some women, and they were followed by a looser and more ragged assortment of hangers-on; children, and older folk, and more of the town's women.

"Can you see Geoffrey?" Cordelia asked Ruby urgently.

"No, my lady. But even if I could … what then?"

The maid had a point. Was Cordelia going to send Ruby down to fetch him out? Unlikely. And not even Cordelia herself now fancied making her way into the crowd herself.

"I wonder what they are going to do," Cordelia said.

And indeed, for a few minutes, it looked as if the rioters themselves did not know what to do. The mill gates were closed to them, and they came up against the stone wall, and for a moment, the sounds of shouting died down.

Into the expectant hush came the Chartist, John Kitt.

200

He must have been at the back, because the people parted and he came walking up through the centre of the crowd. Heads turned towards him, the peaks of the sea of cloth caps all pointing in the direction of the tall, black-clad man. He, unlike the men surrounding him, wore his usual battered black topper.

He swept it from his head as he reached the front of the crowd. The young men at the front eased back and gave him a clear circle to stand in. He waved his hat in the air, and began to speak.

From their vantage point on the hill, they could hear nothing. Cordelia imagined he was speaking of rights, and power, and the common man. Certainly it was firing the imaginations and the passions of the listening crowd; at points, they would all roar together. As his speech went on, the exclamations grew louder.

"I see Geoffrey!" Ruby said. She pointed to the near side of the crowd. "He has his back to us; he's the tall man a few steps to the left of that woman with the pale blue shawl."

Cordelia picked out the shawled woman easily, and used that marker to trace her way to Geoffrey. As soon as she saw him, she recognised him. "We could get to him from here," she said.

"Could," Ruby said. "But we probably shouldn't."

Down below, the crowd was moving now, the people putting their hands in the air again. The group seemed to have got smaller but it was because they were pressing in on one another in their eagerness. Kitt had stopped speaking, or if he was still giving a speech, no one could hear him, because the crowd was roaring.

And then someone threw a stone at a window, and the sound of breaking glass galvanised the whole gathering into a quite terrifying ocean of energy. That one missile unleashed a torrent. Ruby gripped Cordelia's arm and Cordelia let her cling on. They could feel the anger from hundreds of yards away.

The men and women battered on the gates. Some boosted one another up the walls where they sat atop them, throwing more stones into the mill buildings, at the windows, and at the few workers who were present inside.

There were screams, now, but it was impossible to say if they were screams of rage, defiance, or of injury.

The gates were well-bolted. One man jumped down from the wall into the mill courtyard, but something was happening to the crowd. They were moving away from the gates.

Cordelia saw John Kitt again. He clutched his hat in his hand, bare-headed, his black hair tousled in the wind. He strode forward, away from the mill and towards the road. He half looked back over his shoulder, and waved his arm.

The crowd followed, leaving the enthusiastic young man who'd scaled the wall trapped in the mill yard.

"They are going to Mr Welsh's house, my lady!" Ruby said.

"So it seems. What do we do? We can possibly reach his house before they do, and warn him."

"I would imagine that he is already warned," Ruby said. "And look — behind the crowd — here comes the cavalry."

"At last!" Cordelia cried, quickly followed by "Oh no!"

For the mounted soldiers did not slow their pace as they approached the gathering of people. Everyone turned, alerted by the sounds of hooves and blowing horns.

Because the crowd had moved around, the first people that the soldiers came upon were a mix; mainly women and children, but also some of the younger men with their sticks and shovels and poles. They waved them in the air and some of the horses ploughed to one side, but could not stop, due to the men coming up behind them on yet more horses.

Now there was screaming again and it *was* of injury and fury mixed.

At the head of the Hussars rode the glinting, gleaming figure of Captain Percy Slatters. He drew his sword, and raised his hand in the air. The soldiers stopped, and the crowd stumbled backwards.

When all was quiet, Percy sheathed his sword again, and drew out a large sheet of paper from his coat pocket. The crowd pressed together, mumbling.

"He is reading the Riot Act," Cordelia said in a low voice. "Does he have the authority to do so?"

"He has the weapons, and I think that's enough," Ruby said.

Both of them understood the implications of what they were witnessing. If any of the protesters remained there after one hour had elapsed, they were automatically guilty of an offence.

An offence punishable by death.

CHAPTER NINETEEN

Cordelia watched as Percy Slatters tucked the paper away. He sat straight in the saddle and looked around, clearly expecting everyone to disperse immediately.

Like an actor appearing from a hidden trapdoor on stage, a figure rose up. It was John Kitt, borne aloft by some wide-shouldered men, so that he towered above the crowd. His back was to Cordelia and Ruby, but his gestures were unmistakeable.

They were the frantic and accusing gestures of defiance.

The crowd murmured and pressed in closer to one another. Fists were pumped in the air. She could hear jeers, and shouts growing louder.

Percy responded by waving his arms, and standing slightly up in his stirrups. The yeomanry around him grew restless, their horses dancing to and fro.

"He cannot attack yet," Ruby whispered.

"No one is leaving…" Cordelia said.

"Still, he cannot … he must not."

"Oh, I cannot bear to watch this," Cordelia said. She wavered. A foolish part of her wanted to march right down there and send everyone home.

But as fierce as she knew she was, she also knew she'd only end up in worse trouble. Some things simply couldn't be overcome by a loud voice and a decent set of undergarments.

The crowd continued to shout. The yeomanry edged backwards and formed up in a line. Then John Kitt jumped down from the shoulders of the men he was on, and disappeared briefly into the gathering.

He reappeared at the edge of the crowd, on the side closest to Cordelia and Ruby. He looked down the road, and then waved his arm, encouraging everyone to follow him.

"He's still intent on going to Mr Welsh's house!" Ruby said.

Now the cavalry were behind the crowd which was moving away, and roaring as it did so, and Cordelia felt a dread intent in their rising noise.

"Let us get to higher ground," she said, and Ruby needed no urging. They scrambled up the rough hill to watch the mob pass by below. She caught sight of Geoffrey again, at the edge. She wanted to call out to him, urge him to leave the trouble he was striding into.

The yeomanry split, and cantered their horses to either side of the crowd, trying to get before them and prevent them from reaching Simeon's house. The horses were forced to choose between the hillside and riding through the stragglers at the edges of the crowd, and it was inevitable that there were going to be injuries. A woman screamed, and a boy began to shout.

It was enough to turn the mood from repressed menace to overt violence.

It all began to happen so quickly, like a pan suddenly bubbling over. Stones were thrown, and sticks hurled, and horses reared, and the weak sun now flashed on the steel of drawn swords.

Cordelia shouted before she realised she had decided to do so. "Geoffrey! *Geoffrey!*"

He didn't hear her. That was impossible. But he was already running off, at a diagonal to the road, with a few others who were escaping the escalation of horror.

Not enough of the crowd were sensible enough to flee. There was no way that an hour had passed since Percy had read the Riot Act, but the attacks that some of the crowd had made on the soldiers was enough to unleash their fury, and now Cordelia could see blood and she pressed her hand to her mouth, thoroughly sickened.

Ruby pulled at Cordelia's arm. "My lady, we must go, and we must go now. We can do nothing here except gather fuel for nightmares."

Her maid spoke the truth. Cordelia and Ruby linked arms, not mistress and servant, but simply two saddened women, as they made their way through the chill damp air, back to Four Trees.

* * *

Stanley ran out to meet them as they reached the manor house. There ensued five minutes of panicked gabbling from all sides. Then Cordelia and Ruby went into the house, and Cordelia took the shotgun from Stanley to bring with her inside. Stanley hared off in the direction of the mob.

She urged him to stay with them, but he stammered out his need to find Geoffrey, and Cordelia wanted to know that her coachman was safe, so she did not force the matter. She was, however, deeply uneasy while Stanley was away.

Ruby dashed off to the kitchens to relay the events to the cook and to Kate. Cordelia divested herself of her outdoor garments and went directly to the sitting room without changing her walking dress. She knew that Maude would need to know what had been happening.

She explained the events in a bland and dressed-down way, leaving out the part about the mob moving towards her brother-in-law's house. Maude read between the lines, and it pained Cordelia to see her so afraid.

Eventually Stanley returned, bringing with him more things to worry about. "I could not locate Geoffrey, my lady," he said, and his eyes were rolling with panic. "They said he ran off and I went to the town but he was not there."

"Was he injured, do you think? Where is the nearest infirmary?"

"I do not think that anyone has been taken to a hospital," Stanley said. "There are … there are bodies on the ground, and they are being seen to, but I did not see him amongst them." He was pale and sweating. "Nor was he taken prisoner."

"Are you sure?"

He nodded decisively. "Absolutely, my lady. Only one has been taken into custody. There is a lock-up, at the far end of town, and little used until now. I was told that the smith keeps a pig in it, but they have turned the pig out, and now it has a prisoner within."

"Who?" Cordelia asked, even as she was sure she knew the answer.

"John Kitt, my lady."

CHAPTER TWENTY

Maude refused to have any talk of the riot in her presence. It infuriated Cordelia beyond belief. There was little enough to talk of, as it was. But Maude insisted that she be allowed to "live out her dotage in peace" and it was her house — and her rules.

Cordelia began to see that if Maude left to live with Simeon, she would be exposed to more of the world than she wanted to be. And she would have no power over it.

There was to be a small Christmas soiree at Simeon's house in a few days' time, on Friday. Maude spoke of that, but again, she was not interested in gossip. Cordelia decided that she was only going so that she could enjoy the food.

News came from town, piecemeal, brought by the butcher and a boy delivering letters and Kate and Stanley. It was true: only John Kitt had been arrested. And mercifully, there had been no deaths. It was not another

Peterloo. Many were injured, but these were said to be "light injuries." Even so, Cordelia thought, as she made her way to the kitchens that morning, any injury which prevents a person from working will bring more hardship and poverty on that person's family.

Ruby was emerging from the kitchens as Cordelia approached. "Ah, my lady, cook says that you ordered a pie to be made. Are you returned once more to your cookery book?"

Cordelia hadn't even drafted out an article. She had almost forgotten about it. She shook her head. "No, Ruby. Is the pie ready? I am going to take it to the constable."

Ruby's delicate eyebrows shot up. "What?" Then she caught herself and composed her face. "I beg your pardon, my lady. But…"

"I need to know what is happening. Iris is in one place, and John Kitt another. What of Lizzie? What is going on? I hope that I will see the Justice himself at Simeon's soiree on Friday but that is days away. So, I am using these feminine wiles that you speak of, Ruby." Cordelia smiled at Ruby's horrified expression. "But as I lack a slender waist and I can't get the hang of fluttering my eyelids without feeling a little nauseous, I shall have to use the other way to appeal to a man."

"Food."

"Food," Cordelia said, and swept past Ruby to collect the waiting pie.

Ruby followed her into the kitchen. "The last time we saw him, he was … you know. He's a forceful man. I worry … I mean, my lady, this is a bad idea."

"This is the *only* idea," Cordelia said.

"I cannot agree to this." Ruby's words were not of a servant. They were almost like a parent. They fell between them and dropped to the floor.

Cordelia stopped, stunned by the tone, and glared at her maid.

Ruby swallowed. Her face showed that she realised she had not only stepped over the line, she had danced way beyond it, virtually flicking unsavoury gestures at her mistress.

But the maid was as stubborn as she was unwise. Ruby dropped her eyes, but very slowly, slowly enough to make it very plain that she did not want to apologise, and anything forced from her would be false.

Cordelia felt saddened. She told herself she ought to feel angry at her servant's transgression but she felt lost at the sudden lack of support.

She could not sort it out now — she did not have the time — and she would not pursue the argument as it would give legitimacy to the idea that Ruby was allowed to have an opinion. There should be no debate. Maude was right. Cordelia had caused this insurrection by her leniency. She picked up the warm pie dish. It would be a comforting thing to cling to on the walk to town. She said, through gritted teeth, "Get to my room and wait there. I shall deal with you later, as I see fit."

* * *

Cordelia ached with the knowledge that Ruby had taken against her. She expected loyalty and support from her staff. But she also could recognise that the unusual demand she'd put on them had changed their relationship, and really, Cordelia could only blame herself for that. She had expected more … and maybe not given as much as she ought to have given back. She wanted Ruby to be real, to be human, but also to be a doting and unquestioning servant. How could that ever work?

But she could not change things now; too much had happened and too much had been said. And Cordelia would miss the friendship if it withered, now — for friendship it was, of a sort — that she enjoyed with Ruby, unconventional though it was. After all, what other friends did she have? Some members of society shunned her, and other parts accepted her, but she knew that was simply because she amused them. She was a novelty dinner party guest, nothing more. There was enough of a hint of scandal attached to her since that business at Hugo Hawke's to make her interesting and a little dangerous.

Ruby was her closest female friend. It took the threat of loss to show that. Cordelia hugged the warm pie dish to her chest and walked on, grimly.

* * *

The maid at the inn was now a friendly ally. She willingly told Cordelia where she might find Kennett, and directed her to a small but clean-looking house in the town where he lodged in a few rooms on the second floor. The housekeeper showed Cordelia into a dark and oppressive parlour, and went to fetch the constable.

While she waited, Cordelia went to the windows and pulled back the curtains. The glass panes were small and didn't let much light through. *Everything here is so dark*, she thought. *Even the stone is blackened.*

"Well, hello, Lady C, what a marvellous and should I say surprising visit…"

She turned and glared. "Constable Kennett. May I remind you of my correct title? I appreciate that many people in the more rural areas may not have encountered folk such as I, but I had expected that someone like you would have more experience with the world…"

Her flattery worked. He was not so drunk as to be immune to it. He flushed a little, and apologised profusely.

She let him run on a little, and then smiled demurely. "It is I who ought to be apologising to you," she said, and waved her gloved hand at the pie she had placed on the table. "That little misunderstanding when I came to the inn … naturally this is but a small token, but a magnanimous man such as yourself will appreciate the gesture, I am sure."

He could hardly say "no." While she had him on the back foot, she pressed on, and asked about John Kitt's arrest. "For I know that I can receive nothing but the truth from a man like you," she added, wondering at what point she would be over-egging it.

Not yet, clearly. He puffed out his chest and began to speak. "Well, the matter of that poor girl's murder may soon be resolved, and I cannot go into all the details of the investigation, and so on, as your head would soon spin with my technical language."

I doubt it. But she nodded encouragingly.

"However, as a curious fact, we were inclining to bring Captain Slatters to answer some questions *vis a vis* his relationship, or not, with the deceased girl. Forgive me alluding to such indecorous things in your presence, *Lady Cornbrook*. But then — no doubt you have heard of the terrible matters that occurred here yesterday? The lower orders took it upon themselves to make demands! They did!"

You are the lower orders, she thought. "I have heard."

"It was all stirred up by the odious rebel, Kitt. Now we have him in custody and things are falling into place! He is to be held to account. He had been allowed to run amok, as he pleases, for too long. He has been imprisoned before, for distributing seditious literature. He was for transportation, you know, but he used his weasel words and got free after only a few years. This time, my lady, he shall hang!"

"For his part in yesterday's riot?"

"Undoubtedly. And our esteemed Justice thinks he was likely to have been responsible for the murder, too, so we shall be killing two birds with one stone, as it were, if you will pardon the unfortunate phrase."

"But that's obscene. What evidence is there that he even knew Lizzie?"

"They were seen together. We have a witnesses. Indeed, Lizzie herself reported his more seditious tracts to us. And he was inclined to press himself upon her, by all accounts, and who knows what his wicked intentions were! Your dear aunt herself told me, well, she told Mr Gold, and I am of course his representative, that Kitt had made his unsavoury presence felt at her house, too."

"All this is true, yet…"

Kennett talked over her. "A man like Kitt is certain to

217

have committed all manner of heinous crimes that we can only guess at. We should hang him to save time! And mark my words — we shall see no more murders now he is off the streets!"

"Evidence—"

She knew she was fighting a losing battle. It would be nice and neat if Kitt were tried for murder as well as inciting the riot; it would tie it all up and that would be that. She saw that this was the ideal solution for the local Justice of the Peace.

And now Kennett was advancing upon her once more. "I shall ring for some sherry to refresh you," he was saying. "You have travelled far and I want to show you how much I appreciate this gift…"

She straightened her hat and drew back. "Thank you; sadly I have business to attend to. Enjoy the pie. And good day."

* * *

Cordelia strode briskly. The light rain had become sleet now, and she pulled her furs up around her neck. Although she did not enjoy walking in such foul conditions, she focussed on the pleasant sensation of getting back to the house, and changing her clothes, and bundling herself up in front of a fire with a hot drink.

With her stout boots and many layers, and extravagant

muff for her hands, she was in a better position than many she passed on the streets. There were fewer people abroad than usual, which she put down to a combination of the aftermath of the riot, and the inclement weather. Those that had been caught out were running for cover as the sleet intensified and the sky darkened.

People looked at her as she went past. She was a familiar enough sight, now, and her unusual activities had drawn attention since she had arrived. She had been seen entering the inn; she was noted for walking around alone, as she was doing this moment.

Her rejection of the norms emboldened others to look upon her rather than turn away respectfully. A small boy came running up alongside her. He wore wooden clogs and his flapping trousers had holes through which she could glimpse blue skin.

"My lady," he said in his broad accent. "It's reight parky out and silin too! Tha mun let us find thee someone as will tek thee home."

She translated quickly in her head. "No, thank you; I can walk."

"Are tha not starved?"

"I am a little hungry but I shall be home presently."

"Nay, not clemmed. Ah mean starved wi' the cold."

"Oh. No. But goodness, you look like you are. Go

home!" She dug into her bag and found a coin at the bottom. It was not much, but it made the boy's face light up.

"Tha's allus at t'inn," he remarked, still bounding alongside her.

"I wish to discover who killed Lizzie McNab."

"That lass were up at t'Ally Cross?"

"The same," Cordelia said. "Did you know her?"

"Nay, Ah did not. They reckons as John Kitt as did it."

"They? The people of the town?"

"Nay, not us, like. Them." He nodded vaguely but she understood him to mean the Justice and the constable.

"And what do you and your folk believe?" she asked.

"Dunno," he said. "'Cept that Ah don't reckon we'll have no justice now."

"You will. She will," Cordelia said firmly. "I made a promise to my maid that I would find Lizzie's killer."

The boy looked disappointed. "To your maid? What sort of promise is that?"

"One I shall keep."

The boy shrugged, and darted away. *He will soon be regaling his fellows with tales of how strange I am*, she thought, and picked up her pace as she left the town.

She did not believe that John Kitt had anything to do with it.

220

CHAPTER TWENTY-ONE

Cordelia and Maude ate a silent, pensive lunch together. As Kate cleared the things away at the end, Maude said, "You are still set on this murder, are you not?"

"I am. I am sorry, dear aunt. I promise I shan't vex you with talk of it."

"Huh. Well, as to that, I am minded to side with the Justice and hang John Kitt and there is an end of it. When do you return to your house?"

"Am I outstaying my welcome? I intend to leave, as I always planned, the Tuesday before Christmas."

"I do enjoy you being here," Maude said. "Yet I confess I find the company generally to be … well, more wearing than I had expected." But she smiled. "Still, that is my fault and not yours. Yet trouble seems to follow you, Cordelia, and you encourage it."

Cordelia was shocked silent. She could not reply.

"Anyway, do stay for our Christmas get-together at Simeon's. You had promised you would come to this. It can be your farewell gathering."

"Of course." While they were chatting amiably, Cordelia took the chance to ask a question which had been preying on her mind. "Aunt, did you write to Lizzie's family?"

Maude sucked in her cheeks, but she answered, an edge to her voice. "Of course I did. I sent word to her brother and also her sister. Both are married, with families of their own, and frankly they seem to care not what happens to their younger sibling. The sister replied with a short note which directed me to a bank which would furnish the money for a funeral."

"She hasn't been buried yet, has she?"

"The coroner will order it soon enough. Though I sent Simeon to the bank on my behalf — yes, you look surprised, but I have been getting on with things, while you have been gadding about — and the bank told him there was barely enough set aside for a pauper's burial. We shall supplement it, of course. And there you have it."

"Thank you."

Maude snorted. "It was only my duty, no more and no less."

Cordelia begged her leave and withdrew.

* * *

Ruby was brooding in their shared room. She sat curled in the armchair, looking every inch a sullen young girl. Cordelia sat opposite her and poked at the fire for a moment.

Ruby remained silent.

"Ruby, I know that you spoke out of concern."

The maid mumbled, "My lady." It was a default answer for a servant, ambiguous in its meaning.

The poker was heavy in Cordelia's hands. *Discipline*, she told herself. *Maintain distance. Set the boundaries. People are happier with boundaries. We need delineation, we need rules.* Make Ruby understand that though she spoke from a place of genuine worry, her manner of speaking was inappropriate, and other servants had been let go for less. Why, in many households, the maids would spin around and face the wall when the family passed by. Servants were supposed to be invisible.

All those things and more went through Cordelia's head.

She said, "Ruby, I am sorry."

Ruby glanced up. She bit her lip, and looked away almost immediately. "My lady," she repeated.

Cordelia stood up and left the room.

* * *

She wanted to kick things as she went out into the courtyard. Time was running out. She wanted to leave, and she wanted to stay. Why *was* she staying? She wanted her aunt to take on a new companion, or move in with Simeon, but she saw, now, that this was impossible. Maude would not give up her independence, and it was clear that she had not got on well with her previous companion. Indeed, it seemed a relief to Maude that Lizzie was dead—

Cordelia stopped. Surely not? She stood still, halfway to the stables, and a tightness gripped her chest. Perhaps it was the cold air.

Perhaps it was the dawning realisation that the most obvious suspect was her aunt.

"My lady, good afternoon." Geoffrey startled her out of her unwilling speculations. He was in a stable, leaning his arms on the half-door. He seemed to be part of the shadows behind him.

"Ah, Geoffrey! You're back."

"Yes." His craggy, weathered face was inscrutable.

She marched up to him. "Listen. I value you very much as my man, and as my late husband's man before me, but we need to establish some clearer rules."

One eyebrow twitched. He said nothing, but his silence was not one of servile acquiescence.

"I had requested that you stay behind at Clarfields. You

know that I did not do this out of spite; I simply wanted to ensure that your injured leg recovered."

He shrugged. "Sciatica, my lady, and it won't go away so I may as well carry on as I always do."

"Sciatica? Even so — well, never mind. Now, will you tell me where you have been these past few days?"

"You know very well, my lady."

She wanted to stamp her foot. "I want to hear it from your mouth."

His broad hands tightened their grip on the lip of the stable door. He cocked his head. "I was at the protest, at the start of it. Then I left."

He told the truth and she had to give him credit for that. "It is a dangerous business to be mixed up in."

"Yes, my lady."

"We are leaving soon," she went on. "Tuesday, no later. No matter what else happens."

His eyes briefly widened. "So, you believe it was John Kitt as killed the girl? You will walk away from it all?"

"No, I don't believe he did. But we must go home. I cannot fathom it out. It is not my place to do so…"

"If not you, then who?" he said, then shook himself, and continued with a more weary tone. "As you wish, my lady."

First Ruby, now him. Cordelia said, "I am sorry. I am no

detective. This is out of my sphere. And furthermore, my aunt has tired of us, and I must return to prepare Clarfields for Christmas."

"We can't go yet."

"I have told you, we must—"

"The travelling chariot is broken, my lady."

"Is it not repaired yet? I was told you had engaged the smith."

"Yes. But there is work to be done on the axle."

"How can it be taking so long? This is madness."

"I am not a smith. I cannot explain his art."

He met her gaze. He never would look at the ground as he ought to do. "How has it broken?" she demanded. "It was fine on the journey here, and we have barely used it since."

"Perhaps it was trusting to that boy to drive you, my lady."

"Stanley is a good and careful man!"

"He's a boy and knows little. He aims for potholes."

Stanley had been frantic when he thought you injured in the riot, she thought. *You don't deserve his idolisation.* "He would grow into his place better if you set a finer example," she said. "I intend to make a coachman of him. And you would be mindful to remember your place."

She hated saying it, but there it was. She had had to

discipline Ruby and now Geoffrey. She would claw back control of her staff. Geoffrey stiffened and inclined his head almost imperceptibly.

Cordelia spun on her heel. Somewhere in a nearby room, a head moved backwards from a window and disappeared into the darkness. She looked up at the long manor house and a curtain on the first floor twitched and fell straight.

They were all watching her; all of her staff. They all wanted something from her. Money, security, justice even.

She could have jumped on a horse, in that moment, and ridden away from it all.

CHAPTER TWENTY-TWO

That evening, Cordelia tried to broach yet another difficult subject with Maude. The sleet had stopped but the air was chill. They huddled together in the sitting room. Maude had asked Cordelia to read from a book and it had been heavy going; it was a dull sort of novel, the type that delivered important and improving messages to the reader. There was a distinct lack of rippling Dukes striding across ballrooms to claim their young brides. *What was the point of a book without that*, Cordelia thought.

When she finally reached the end of an interminable chapter in which nothing had happened but the heroine having a bit of a cry, then praying, she closed the book and said, "My dear aunt. I have some news which is going to shock you, but I think it will also bring you some comfort. I have discovered why you are not sleeping as well as you might."

Maude looked up in curiosity. "Go on, my dear."

"I … spoke with Iris Fletcher. I wished to see if I might bring her comfort in her current state of imprisonment. And she confessed to me that your sad erstwhile companion was administering laudanum to you, at night, so that you slept soundly while she went off to—"

"No!" Maude threw up her wrinkled hand. "Tell me no more! I can imagine full well what that fallen maid was off and doing. I do not even wish to hear her name spoken in that way. We spoke of her this morning and my connection to her is over."

"But this explains, does it not, why now you struggle to sleep?"

"It does," Maude conceded. "Good riddance. I was going to let her go after Christmas anyway. It was only Christian charity that stopped me from doing so before the holiday, knowing that her brother and sister would not take her in."

"Even so, her life was—"

"I said *enough*," Maude said firmly. "Now, have you decided what you will wear on Friday, for the gathering at Simeon's? A woman of your … stature … must dress carefully if you are not to appear mannish. And as a widow, of course, your colours are limited."

"I am out of mourning. I can wear whatever colour I

choose."

"I don't think so, dear. You can never be as you once were, unless you marry again."

Cordelia wanted to roll her eyes. She bit her tongue, and let Maude explain, at length, all the things that were wrong with Cordelia's life.

* * *

The walk to town that morning should have been enough for Cordelia, but when she retired to her rooms later, she still felt restless and ill at ease. Maude had taken to her bed early, and Cordelia was not sleepy. There was no sign of Ruby, and Cordelia did not care to hunt for her. Things had not yet returned to their normal easy conversation between them, yet. Instead, she put on her plainest, roughest gown and wrapped up in a shawl that Ruby had left out on a chair. She had a mind to go wandering, and she didn't want to look like a rich target. A poor woman might have all the freedom of the land, she thought as she crept out of the manor house and into the strangely still night. All the freedom with none of the power or money to do anything with that freedom.

And freedom to be attacked, and killed, she reminded herself. *I shan't be heading up to the Ally Cross.* And if she did not go that way, then her options were limited. She could not walk the paths of the moorland in the night, even though many were of laid flagstones and causeys. Her only choice was to head towards town. The moon was near full, and lit everything with its anaemic glow. The road was easy to follow.

She only intended to go a few hundred yards, enough to relax and bring some peace to her. But her feet took her onwards until she was approaching the town itself. She stopped a little distance away.

It seemed such a quiet and peaceful place. Perhaps it was due to the lack of wind, and the almost-empty street. She surveyed the town until she started to grow cold. She knew she ought to turn around and go home.

Perhaps I could go into the inn and order a drink, she thought, a frisson running down her spine. She began to head along the main street, pulling the shawl over her head and tucking it around her face.

No. Even with this, they will recognise me, she reminded herself. *I can't disguise my voice well enough. And anyway, I have brought no money with me.*

She slowed, and stood on the road outside the inn, looking up at the warmly glowing yellow lights in the windows.

From this close, she could hear laughter and music and shouting. It made her feel even more excluded, all of a sudden. She was drawn closer. She wanted to look inside.

She rose up on tip-toes and put her hands on the stone ledge below the window, craning her neck. She could see Percy Slatters, and he was sitting on the bar — not at it, but literally on the polished wooden counter top. He had a tankard in his hand, and splashes of liquid down his unbuttoned jacket. He was laughing. His booted feet were up on a stool, and he was surrounded by a gaggle of men, and one or two slatternly-looking women who were far too underdressed for the current weather conditions.

The window panes were thin and she could hear what many of them were saying, although it was all jumbled together with laughter and shouting. It was obvious that Percy was the hero of the hour. As she looked more closely, she noticed that the ones surrounding him were soldiers and easy women.

All the workers were drawn off to one side, and they were not toasting the cavalryman at all.

But she doubted that he cared for their opinions. He was crowing like a cockerel atop the bar, and had his pick of drink and women for this night and likely many more to come.

She pulled her shawl tighter, turned and headed for home.

CHAPTER TWENTY-THREE

Cordelia went straight back up to the inn on Thursday morning before her breakfast eggs had even settled in her belly. Ruby came with her, but her conversation was restricted to the menial matters of what to prepare for the upcoming party at Simeon's. It was tedious talk, but necessary. Cordelia hoped that her apology was fermenting in Ruby's heart, but she wasn't going to push things too hard. She would let things take their course.

Ruby was then sent off to the haberdasher's while Cordelia entered the inn, nodded at the maid, and headed up to see Iris without asking any leave to do so. The room was locked but unguarded. All Cordelia had to do was turn the key and step within.

Iris was out of bed, and dressed, and appeared to be sticking to her usual daily routines in spite of incarceration. She stiffened as she heard the door, but relaxed — slightly

— when she saw Cordelia.

"Miss Fletcher. How do you do today?"

"No better, my lady."

"Any worse?"

A darkness flitted across the woman's face and she frowned, briefly. She pressed her lips tight shut.

Cordelia took a seat on the end of the hard bed. "Tell me about Percy Slatters, Iris." She switched to her first name, hoping to foster a more informal feeling.

"He is a Captain in the Hussars. He leads the yeomanry here," Iris said in a dull and flat tone.

"You know more than that, do you not?"

Iris looked up, and said, vehemently, "What has that treacherous snake been saying about me? Lies, mark my words. Lies!"

Cordelia waited a moment but Iris lapsed into silence again. She eventually said, "What sort of lies has he spread before, Iris?"

Iris was staring away from her now, as if there was something in the corner of the room. "He has two faces, that man."

"I see a genial, popular army officer; that is one face. What is his other, Iris?"

Iris swayed from side to side, still staring at nothing. "But they hear him," she said. "They hear him say one thing and say another, mean one thing and mean another. You cannot trust him, my lady. I did. I was wrong. I was fooled. But they have removed the scales from my eyes, my lady, and now I see him as he truly is, and I will not be tricked by him again, oh no."

"How did he trick you? Were you lovers?"

The question dropped into the air between them. Cordelia held her breath.

Iris spoke in a small voice like a leaf skittering across a wooden floor. "Yes. For a time. Yes, we were."

Ah, confirmed at last. Cordelia had to ask. "Was this before ... or after ... he was walking out with Lizzie?"

Iris did not answer.

"Or during?"

Still Iris remained silent.

"Iris, listen. This is important…"

"Only so that they can pin more evil slander upon me," she replied. "And they will believe him, not me, will they not? Oh, I heard them all, singing his praises, Captain Slatters, what a man! What a hero! Saving the mill! All he does is ride a fancy horse and wave a sword. And lie. We were supposed to—"

"To what?"

"Have a future." Iris sighed. "At least I know the truth about him, now." She was swaying again.

"Iris, you must tell me, when were you seeing Percy? Will he confirm this?"

Iris stared and swayed and began to hum, a strange low buzzing coming from deep in her chest.

"Please, Miss Fletcher…" But Cordelia could see it was hopeless. Iris wrapped her arms around her body and her eyes focused on nothing but empty air. Cordelia got up and left, and she did not think that Iris even noticed that she had gone.

* * *

The matter of the broken axle played on Cordelia's mind all the way back to Four Trees. She did not enter the house. She skirted around and found Stanley sweeping the yard.

"Tell me," she said without preamble. "Is that chariot of ours fixed yet?"

Stanley swept the broom ferociously over the same patch of dusty ground, over and over. "I think it is not, my lady."

"And what exactly is the problem?"

"A broken axle."

"And the smith was engaged to fix it?"

"I believe he was, my lady. He came to see it. But Geoffrey dealt with him."

"I cannot understand why it is not fixed. We have the

238

funds. And tell me something else, Stanley. How did it break in the first place?"

"Well, Geoffrey says that it was how I drove too harshly over the potholes."

"He says, does he? And what do you say?"

Stanley stopped sweeping. He kicked at a stone. "My lady, I … he is very knowledgeable and I respect his opinion."

"But he's wrong, isn't he?"

Stanley stammered so badly she could not make out his reply, and he ground to a halt as Geoffrey emerged from the tack room. He strode towards Cordelia.

"Ah, Geoffrey. Tell me more about how the chariot's axle broke."

"The lad been spouting off, has he?"

"No, Geoffrey, I want to know how it really broke. Because I am starting to think that it might not have been an accident." As soon as she said it, she realised it was the most likely explanation.

"Not an accident?" Geoffrey said, and snorted. "Don't give the lad enough credit to be taking on sabotage."

"Not him. You."

He tried to laugh. "Why would I do that?"

"To make a point. To prove something. To get back at me because you are all in with the Chartists now. To show

239

how fed up you were that I left you behind. To keep us here for whatever reason."

"Keep us here? Ha! No, the axle broke in an accident."

"Stanley said—"

Geoffrey turned away from her, and she was shocked by his rudeness. "Well, if the lad knows so much, let him deal with it. You don't need me, apparently. Let him see to it, and let's see where you are then."

And he walked away.

CHAPTER TWENTY-FOUR

Cordelia knew it was an act of sabotage by Geoffrey. His reaction confirmed it, and even gave her the suspicion as to the reason why.

"Let him deal with it," he had said.

He has had his nose put out of joint, she thought. *And this stems right from the beginning, when I left him at Clarfields to come here without him. He cannot see that I did it for him. All he feels is abandoned. So he's turned to John Kitt and found a new fire, and he has damaged the coach to prove to me how much he needs me.*

But she had no evidence.

So she decided to go to the lock-up in town. She wanted to talk to John Kitt, and she also wanted to talk to the smith about Geoffrey; as Kitt was currently being held in the smith's pig sty, it would be a good chance for her to do both of these things.

Thursday was another cold day but the sky was a

brilliant blue. Ice and frost had formed overnight. She walked through the town and people directed her to the smith's forge at the far end. She turned up a track between two rows of low cottages. The ground had frozen hard in rough lumps, jagged bits of mud and soil creating difficult terrain to walk over, even with good boots. At the far end was a gate, pulled shut. She looked over the gate to see a courtyard surrounded on three sides. The furthest side was a house, and to the right were some stables and an outbuilding with large doors; the forge, she assumed. To the left was a lower building, with one small square window and a door only four feet high. There was a roughly made fence of stout wood and panels around this small building.

And held in by the fence was an enormous pig.

She unlatched the gate and it swung open easily, the well-made hinges a testament to the smith's craft. She was sure to close it carefully behind her.

First she went to the building on her right and peeped in through the half-open door, but all she could see within was the glowing embers of a fire in a chimney, and nothing else but shadows.

She went to the house and knocked, but there was no reply.

So she found herself leaning on the panelled fence and looking at a large pig. It was white with black, irregular

242

spots, and it was very hairy. She thought it unusual to see; most people would kill their household pig for the winter. There was no point feeding an animal when that animal could be feeding the family.

Maybe it was a good breeder, she thought. It was a sow, and it was as interested in Cordelia as she was with the pig. The pig's little eyes were mostly covered by flappy triangular ears but it cocked its head and peered up at Cordelia.

Goodness, she thought. *This thing is large enough for a child to ride.*

She had never been this close to a pig before. Of course, as a countryside gentlewoman, she was used to horses, dogs and all manner of dead game; but this was a farming thing, and well beyond her remit. She tentatively reached down to scratch the pig's head. It grunted. *Was that a good sign? Did they have teeth? Were they territorial?*

She looked past the pig to the door. It had two bolts, top and bottom. "Hey!" she called, and then again, more loudly. "Hey! John Kitt, are you within?"

There was no reply from the outbuilding, but behind her, a man started to laugh.

She whirled around. "Are you the smith?"

"Aye. I am," he said. His accent was not as broad as most of the locals she had met, and nor did he quite meet the stereotype of the big, burly blacksmith that she had in her head. He was short, and not the barrel-chested behemoth of popular legend. Instead he seemed tough, sinewy and of a muscular leanness. His hair was sandy but he was thin on top, she noticed, as he briefly doffed his cloth cap. "Adam Revesley at your service. And what might that be, madam? Your service, I should say."

"I am looking for John Kitt."

"I wondered as to why you were calling him. Well, so you found him, but he is there under lock and key for the authorities. He is a dangerous man."

"May I speak to him?"

"Nay, you mayn't." He smiled pleasantly but he folded his arms, and rested his weight on one foot. He was not a man to meddle with, she could see that. There was an air of education about him. There were myths about such folk, she remembered. Smiths were not as other trades.

She didn't think it would do much good but she tried to use her name anyway. "I am Cordelia, Lady Cornbrook," she said. "I have an especial interest in this matter as my aunt, Miss Stanbury, lost her companion to that dreadful murder; and Mr Kitt stands accused, so I believe."

The smith shrugged. "As to that, I don't know. He is a trouble maker, though," he added, and smiled as if he had sympathies.

"Indeed," she said. "I cannot disagree. Now, can I see

244

him?"

"No."

What did he want? She wondered if she could bribe him. Would that insult him? He obviously wasn't poor enough to have to kill his pig.

He broke into her thoughts by saying, "I can see you don't know what to do. I shall tell you this, then. If you can get to the door then you can get in to speak to him. Look, here I shall even give you the key." He pulled a large iron loop from a nail on the wall by the sty. It was but a few feet from the low door, but might as well have been a mile, for all the good it could do John Kitt on the inside.

"Oh, for goodness sake!"

He grinned, unrepentant. "I do like a laugh."

"Will that — your pig — injure me? That will not go down well with the Justice."

"Nor will trespass," he replied. "Nay, she'll not injure you, I don't think."

"Don't think?"

He shrugged again, and pointed to the corner of one fence panel. "You can go in that way. Should I hold your muff?"

"I don't care for your hands anywhere near my muff," she replied sniffly, and stepped to the corner of the fence.

There was no gate, as such. She could see that the

panels were simply lifted away to allow access, so she chose the corner which had arced scuff marks in the frozen ground. She pulled at it, bringing it an inch from the ground.

Instantly the sow was there, her heavy head nudging at the gap that Cordelia had just created. The pig began to push.

"Don't let her escape now," the smith warned.

Cordelia let the fence panel drop, and shoved it with her hip to close it up again. She leaned over, and tried to shoo the pig away. "Get off, now! Get away with you!"

The pig's snout tilted upward.

"This is hopeless," she said. She turned to see the smith. "What can I do, or say, or give you that you might allow me to talk to John Kitt? It is an urgent matter."

"Nowt," he said. "I don't believe any woman, least of all yourself, has any urgent matter with this man."

She wanted to stamp her feet. She gathered herself, lifted her chin, and sailed away, with as much dignity as could be mustered given that she had just taken on a pig, and a smith, and lost.

Halfway home she remembered she had not challenged him on the matter of the broken axle.

CHAPTER TWENTY-FIVE

Simeon had clearly gone to a great deal of trouble to make his house feel warm and welcoming that Friday evening. In spite of the trouble at his mill, and the problems of his workers, and the general unrest, still his grand house was finely decked out with the latest fashions, including a small tree in the large entrance hall, looking utterly dwarfed by the sweeping staircase that rose above it.

He had more staff than Cordelia had expected, or perhaps he had hired in extra for the event. It was, Simeon had claimed, just a small function — a few close friends and local worthies — and that was true. Indeed, the servants in their dark livery almost outnumbered the guests.

This did have the advantage that one's glass was never allowed to be empty.

Simeon declared it to be an evening of music and merriment.

"You do not mean to suggest there might be dancing," the Reverend said with a frosty edge.

Simeon smiled. "Of course not, dear sir; I know full well your objections to the way young men and women can … ahem … press themselves against one another."

The Reverend began to go dark red. "And the movements! Of the hips!"

Goodness, thought Cordelia, moving backwards out of the conversation hastily. *He is a puritan of a very old stripe indeed. No dancing? No doubt he would also turn out to be one of those temperance sorts.* It was a growing tendency for otherwise perfectly sane folk to suddenly stand up and declare that one should not drink spirits. Yet others went even further and pressed for the avoidance of beer and wine too. Though Cordelia had suffered at the hands of her drunken husband, she blamed him; not alcohol. She clutched her glass a little tighter and edged away.

The Justice of the Peace, Mr William Gold, caught sight of her and descended. She attempted to press him into conversation about John Kitt, or Iris Fletcher, or even Lizzie McNab but he was having none of it and refused to converse with her on any topic more controversial than the weather or the decorations that adorned the pleasant parlour.

"You really must leave these questions aside," he told her with a paternalistic tone.

"I have an interest—"

"An unseemly one," he said, and his voice had become more hard-edged and warning. Then he smiled. "Let us talk of more happy matters! Will you still be here for the ball?"

"Which ball?"

"The annual Christmas ball. Not here, of course. Everyone within a thirty-mile radius will be there. This year it is to be held in Harrogate at some very exclusive rooms hired for the occasion. You must have been invited; your aunt has, certainly, and you can come with her." He continued to prattle on, telling her of the Earl of this and the Countess of that, and the titled lady of some repute who was hosting the ball itself. Cordelia vaguely remembered her from her seasons in London, and did not fancy spending time with her.

"I am afraid I return to my own house in the next few days," she said. "By Tuesday, at the latest."

"Of course," he said. "No doubt you have much to do there."

"Indeed." She clammed up. She had received a letter, most unexpectedly, that morning, from her cook Mrs Unsworth. She hadn't even known that Mrs Unsworth could write. She knew she could read, of course, for she had recipes and receipts. Her handwriting was solid and angular, and the pen dug deeply into the paper, roughing it up and tearing small holes. Her spelling was erratic, but the sense was clear.

Mrs Unsworth was virtually instructing her mistress to come home.

There were also allusions to the other members of staff — particularly Ruby and Stanley who were, in Mrs Unsworth's eyes, on a kind of extended holiday while Mrs Unsworth and the other hard workers were slaving away at home. *Just what work do you have while I am not there? But then*, Cordelia reminded herself, *there is a lot about the working classes that I do not know.*

Various other veiled spites and insinuations littered the letter which petered out in a fragmentary sentence: "Anyway geffrey shall see to it all as i have no dowt."

What will Geoffrey see to, exactly? The letter had irked Cordelia. *After all I have done, and I do, for you,* she thought. But then Mrs Unsworth did not know the full extent of Cordelia's involvement in her life, so perhaps some of the old cook's spite was understandable. Without Cordelia's hidden help, Mrs Unsworth would be in an even worse position. It was one more demand that was levied on her, in her position. She sighed.

She wondered about the ragged remnants of Mrs Unsworth's family and had a fresh pang of sympathy for the nasty old baggage.

"A penny for your thoughts!"

"Oh — dear aunt, I am sorry."

"I thought you would be the centre of attention here, tonight, Cordelia."

The wine was making Cordelia both maudlin, and light-headed. She tried to push her musings aside, and she smiled. "I confess I have so much in my head that it is making things difficult for me to simply relax."

"And that is the final proof, if any were needed, that you think far too much."

Cordelia noted her aunt's flushed cheeks and sweet breath. She was drunk. Cordelia's smile widened. "Are you having fun?" she asked.

"I am now I'm on my second glass."

"Goodness me."

"Well," her aunt said, her cheeks puffing out, "it is Christmas, is it not? The Reverend has been giving me sideways looks."

"I expect he will be preaching on the evils of drink this weekend."

"I expect he shall. Now, speaking of matters spiritual, what think you to a séance?"

"Oh no. Not you as well," Cordelia said, surprised at her aunt's sudden turn.

"Me as well as who?"

"Spirits and ghosts and all that; it is an interest of that seamstress, Iris Fletcher."

"Oh," Maude said, waving her hand and spilling her wine slightly. "That silly thing knows nothing. My old friend Catherine suggested it. I told her I was not interested but she has a way of grinding one down, you know? And at my time of life, it does behove one to be a little more aware of what lies beyond the veil, so to speak. I consider it to be a manner of forward planning."

"And what does the Reverend think of this plan?" Cordelia asked.

"Hush, Cordelia. As if I would let him know. I have a great deal of respect for the man when he is in the pulpit."

"But at other times…?"

"Well, let us simply acknowledge that his place *is* the pulpit. Anyway, Catherine and one or two others will be coming around on Sunday afternoon. Do join us."

"I really don't think—"

Cordelia's objection was interrupted by the return of William Gold. "Now, my good lady, what I have warned you about thinking?" He laughed richly and she smiled thinly and politely back at him.

Someone began to play the piano. It was a middle-aged man who launched into a song that had the air of a music hall about it, with references to Saucy Annie and her knickers. The Reverend began to cough frantically, and Simeon glided to the piano-player's side.

With great skill, the song slipped into a ballad about a lost maiden choosing a life of celibacy, penance and prayer. The Reverend took a seat, crossed his legs, and allowed himself to nod.

Cordelia rolled her eyes at her aunt. She was sure that Maude winked back.

CHAPTER TWENTY-SIX

The evening had not lasted late into the night. Cordelia found herself tucked up in her warm bed nice and early; they certainly didn't keep London hours, up here in the wild north. As a consequence, she was awake early on Saturday morning. Ruby had finally thawed out and was speaking to her again. Their relationship was in a newer place, and little by little, the banter was returning. She instructed her maid to begin packing for their return on Tuesday.

"And Lizzie?" Ruby had said.

Cordelia wanted to hang her head. "I've done all I can."

Ruby turned away. Cordelia bit her lip, and then went to the stables to find Stanley or Geoffrey.

"It still is not fixed," Geoffrey said curtly.

"Make it so, or we'll be travelling home in a gig."

"There is not enough room for us all," he said.

"There is not. And for that reason, you shall be running

alongside, like a footman of old. Why, you did tell me you were quite fit and well, did you not?"

He narrowed his eyes, but pulled at his cap in the most disrespectfully slovenly way that he could get away with. She snapped, "And smarten yourself up — if you wish to remain in my service."

"My lady," he said.

She was angry, now. Angry at her own impotence to get anything solved, anything at all. She knew she'd been foolish to suppose that she could discover the truth behind Lizzie's murder. She had brought one killer to justice but that hardly qualified her as some kind of new lady-policeman.

Her feelings of helplessness were compounded by the other issues. By pursuing the murder, she had not managed to make any progress on her proposed culinary articles for journals or magazines, let along write a whole book about the subject. Her relationships with her staff were on shaky and changing ground, and her once-loyal coachman was increasingly under the dangerous sway of the Chartists.

Yet she could see the appeal, for people like Geoffrey and even Ruby, of what the Chartists asked for.

It was against the natural order of things, of course — but then, so was she. She was refusing to marry again, but nor would she retire to a widow's seclusion. She asked questions. She forced herself out into the world. The world pushed back, and she thought that things were growing more strict and more moral with the maturity of Queen Victoria. As the great woman settled into her role, and grew her family, it seemed that the families of England were also changing. By the time that the Queen's uncle, William, had acceded to the throne in 1830, the wild parties of the time of the Prince Regent — later King George IV — were already fading as the fat old King had grown tired, ill and incapable. Now that Victoria sat on the throne, and the world had adjusted to a woman sitting there, a new code of behaviour was starting to creep through the parlours of the country. *Where will it end?* Cordelia thought idly. *Will we all be teetotal and listening to nothing but moral ditties by 1850? I hope not.*

"My lady?"

Her attention jerked back. Stanley was watching her with blunt, honest concern in his wide and watery eyes.

"Ah, Stanley. I need to go into town."

"It's very cold, my lady…"

"Indeed it is. Will you have the gig made ready? You can drive me."

He jumped to it, and she went inside to dress more warmly and appropriately for the journey.

* * *

Her anger took her back to the smith's place. She still had a question for him regarding the axle, and she was determined to speak to Kitt. The gate to the yard was standing open and Stanley drove them right into the courtyard where they wheeled around, and she jumped down. She went first to the forge. The door was open, and the fires were roaring, but again it was empty.

But this time there was someone in the house; Mrs Revesley, the smith's petite and bird-like wife. She had dark hair curled up under her bonnet, and piercingly black eyes. She smiled when Cordelia greeted her, and bobbed a curtsey.

"My husband is away for the moment," she said. "But he shall not be long. I expect him back by midday." Her accent, like the smith's, was not as thick and broad as the other country dwellers of the county. And peeping past her to the interior of the cottage, Cordelia could see books on shelves that lined the walls.

"It is not he that we are here to see," Cordelia said. "I need to speak to John Kitt."

"Oh. Ah. He is locked up, my lady, and he is a dangerous man."

"So I hear. Yet I have met this man on more than one occasion and I believe him to bear me no harm."

Mrs Revesley looked past Cordelia and her hands smoothed down her aprons. "Please, do come in and wait for my husband…"

"I am afraid I have some other pressing engagements. Tell me, Mrs Revesley, how does he fare, out there, in this freezing weather?"

The woman's brow creased, fine lines deepening at the corners of her eyes. "I have provided him with many blankets," she said, and there was an air of confession about it.

"Your husband approves?"

"He does not know."

"I imagine you feed him, also."

"I do," Mrs Revesley said. "For I am not a monster, and my husband is not either, though he is thoughtless about everyday things even if he is a thinker about the big things. So yes, I give John Kitt food, hot food when I can. And I see to it that he is warm in there, and not maltreated. But do you know, my lady, what is to happen to him?"

"Hanging, I am told, but they must bring him to trial."

"When? At the Lent assizes?"

"I think so."

"Well, he cannot stay in our pig sty for months."

"I don't think he will; they will take him to York castle soon enough, I imagine. And from there his fate seems certain."

The smith's wife looked unhappy. "We are told not to

take a life, so why is the punishment for taking a life to also take a life?"

"That is a question for the Reverend, not I," Cordelia said. "Now, my time runs short. I am concerned that though this man is, indeed, a rabble-rouser and riot-raiser, I do not think him to be a murderer, and it is on that count that I wish to talk with him."

"They will hang him for the riot so why not the murder also? Proving him innocent of that will not change his fate."

"Indeed it won't," Cordelia said. Already Mrs Revesley was moving towards the pig sty, and Cordelia followed. "But it means that the real culprit can still be brought to justice."

Mrs Revesley nodded. Cordelia didn't know what part of her argument had swayed the smith's wife, but it didn't matter. It was enough that it had.

"I cannot let you in, of course," Mrs Revesley said. "But I can get old Betty out of the way."

To Cordelia's admiration — and astonishment — Mrs Revesley picked up the whole large panel that made one side of the sow's enclosure, and walked briskly forward. Her tiny frame didn't seem strong enough to hustle the pig to the corner but she did, and the sow grunted and allowed herself to be pressed into a smaller space. Mrs Revesley dropped the panel to the ground again. The pig was now in a triangular section, and the way was clear to the door.

It was that easy. *Huh*, thought Cordelia, *so now I know how to handle a pig. I'll remember that.*

Mrs Revesley drew back to her house, but remained on the doorstep, shivering in the chill wind, as Cordelia rapped sharply on the door to John Kitt's prison.

He called out from within. "Why do you knock? I can hardly let you in. My lady," he added, and from that she knew he was watching her through some crack or knothole.

"Politeness," she answered. "How are you, Mr Kitt?"

"I'm cold and hungry and I'm locked in a pig sty. And how are you … Cordelia?"

"Not to be addressed as Cordelia."

"Even here, even now, you will rigidly adhere to society's conventions? A man learns a lot about himself when he's locked in a small dark room, you know. A man learns that all are equal. We are all flesh and blood and bone, Cordelia."

"Even here," she replied, "for it seems to me that clinging on to the last vestiges of dignity and respect when in such a situation is what marks us out as different from animals and savages."

"I am a savage, then," he said, and began to cough. It was distressing to listen to, but she could not help. She waited for the fit to subside.

"You are not a *murdering* savage, though, are you?" she said.

"Ah, that. Yes, I know they intend to say I killed that girl. She had a high sense of herself, so she did."

"Did you give her your pamphlets to read?"

"Of course I did. She was a simmering cauldron of resentment and hate, you know. Ripe for turning. Ripe for me."

Because she could not see his laughing face, his words were divorced from his good looks and charm, and she felt a ripple of distaste bring the hairs to stand up on her skin. "And did she turn?"

"She would have, given the chance. I needed more time. She could have been my way in, there."

"Way in? To my aunt's house?"

After a pause, he said, "To anywhere."

"What do you mean?"

He began coughing again, and this time the hacking, phlegmatic sounds lasted for over a minute, and she grew concerned. She glanced up at the house, where Mrs Revesley waited, arms folded.

"Do you need water?" she asked as he regained control.

"I need freedom," he said. "Or a fresh blanket, yes, and a jar of water would be welcome. Ale would be even better."

"I will ask. But before I do so, tell me everything you know about Lizzie McNab — and Iris Fletcher. And Percy Slatters. Do you know him?"

"Well, yes, I do ought to know the captain of the yeomanry and the man who brought me down. And the irony of it! Oh, those three. What a web of duplicity they are caught in. And that one especially; one face, then another — oh…" And he was consumed by coughing again.

She could not bear to listen to it. She crossed the yard to Mrs Revesley and asked her for water and a blanket. "He is ill," she said.

"I know it, but I cannot open the door while my husband is not here."

"There are three of us; he will not be able to rush us and escape." She pointed at Stanley, who at that moment was standing hunched by the horse and looking unlikely to even stop a wet paper bag from blowing past him.

"I do not trust him."

But even from across the courtyard, they could both hear his lung-tearing coughs. Mrs Revesley looked pained. She sighed, and went into her house. When she came back out, she was carrying a shotgun, a blanket and a stone bottle with a cork in it. *Ale*, Cordelia thought, *and I don't begrudge him that.*

"Ask your lad to carry the gun," she said, and Cordelia

clicked her fingers to bring Stanley over. She instructed him to train it on the door of the prison.

Mrs Revesley came with Cordelia to the door, and she lifted the ring of keys from the nail. The ring was a single rusted loop, and the three keys on it looked identical. She didn't sort through them; she just pushed the first one into the lock, but before she turned it, she called out.

"Mr Kitt, we have a gun aimed right at you. Go to the back of the cell, and I can give you a blanket and some ale."

He coughed, and spluttered out, "I thank you for your kindness. I am in no state to — to escape." His voice faded slightly.

But when Mrs Revesley swung the door outwards, he was revealed there, far too close, half-standing and leaning against the door jamb, and not at all at the back of the dank, dark room. Mrs Revesley screamed, and pushed the blankets at him, before hastily dropping the bottle and kicking it into the cell.

Cordelia had a brief and confused impression of the bent figure of John Kitt, stooping to see under the four-foot-high lintel, his hands against the door frame as he laughed before the door swung closed. Mrs Revesley's hands were shaking as she frantically tried to lock the door, but the lock was stiff and obviously unused.

But with an effort she pulled the key free. She shouted

264

through the door, "I showed you a kindness! And you mock me for it."

"I am sorry," he replied. "I did not mean to startle you and I meant no harm at all. I appreciate all these things that you do for me. I had no intention of trying to escape. I simply wished to glimpse daylight for a moment…"

Mrs Revesley huffed. She grabbed the fence panel and dragged it back to its original spot, and the sow was released to her full roaming area once more.

Stanley accompanied her back to the house and handed back her gun. Cordelia made a stilted thank you, and let Stanley drive her home.

She wrapped up in blankets and furs, trying to get comfortable on the gig's hard bench. John Kitt had been up to something. She had made sure to check that there were still three keys on the ring when Mrs Revesley had hung it back on the nail. He was not above some sleight of hand, she realised. Why, his whole "illness" might be a feint.

But three keys remained on the ring, and he was locked up once again.

Something troubled her. She could not see it yet.

And he had spoken, also, of duplicity. Whose? All of them — Lizzie, Iris and Percy also?

She closed her eyes and let her daydreams make the connections for her.

CHAPTER TWENTY-SEVEN

For a while, Maude was happy that Cordelia seemed to be in a more appropriate relationship with her maid — that is, Ruby was silent and Cordelia standoffish. Things had thawed now, and Maude was back to her disapproving self.

Ruby had not wanted Cordelia to put herself in danger with Constable Kennett. Cordelia knew that. Ruby was also too conflicted; she wanted justice for Lizzie, as some kind of representative of all working women, but she also — quite simply — wanted to go home.

And Cordelia wondered, also, if there was not an element of disappointment hanging around the lady's maid. Cordelia felt that in some strange way she had let Ruby down by not catching the killer of Lizzie. And by letting Ruby down, she was letting down all the defenceless young woman who suffered at the hands of men.

Oh, this is ridiculous, she told herself. *I am overthinking this! It does not have to be one thing or another. Why, half the time, we act without even knowing our own motives. Who knows why Ruby is as she is? I would wager she does not know herself.*

Cordelia stood at the fire, and contemplated dressing for bed. It was not so very late, but there was nothing else to do. She could curl up and read, with a hot drink at her side.

Ruby sat opposite her, a piece of needlework in her hands. She had turned, in her boredom, to attempting a sampler. So far she had made a neat straight line of green across the bottom. Four hours later, and that was still her total achievement.

"What do you intend it to show?" Cordelia asked.

Ruby scowled, at her work not at her mistress. "I thought at first I'd do a cottage and a field of flowers around it."

"How beautiful."

"Now I think I might recreate the Battle of Hastings instead."

"Oh. That's quite a change."

"I have stabbed my thumb so many times that I could make use of the blood stains," Ruby said.

"You are a competent seamstress!"

"For plain sewing. This is a whole new world." Ruby

folded the fabric up and threw it to lie on top of her workbasket, where it unfolded itself and slithered to the floor. Ruby sighed, and sat back.

"Ruby, would you run to the kitchens and bring me a hot toddy that I might drink in bed?"

"Yes, my lady."

Ruby disappeared, and Cordelia paced to the window, twitching the curtain aside to peer into the dark and foggy night. She could see a darkness, a blacker shadow in the grey and black swirling mist.

It's just my eyes playing tricks, she thought. *I've been looking at the flames of our fire. It's the way that tree is moving.*

Wait. Her breath froze. *There are no trees at Four Trees. And anyway — trees don't move.*

There is someone out there. It is a man. It's not Maude, this time. Cordelia could see that he was tall, and he walked carefully but confidently, and then he stopped and seemed to be looking up at the house. The fog thickened and thinned randomly, and it gathered around him, making him seem to recede without moving. He turned, and brought his hand up, and she could see a glow. He had a lantern or a torch. Then he stepped backwards, definitely, and the fog took him.

She was about to move away when another movement caught her eye. This was a figure emerging from the house;

she could see him from above, just the top of his battered hat, and the long thin shape of a shotgun or maybe a rifle. She recognised him immediately.

It was Geoffrey, and he was striding towards the spot that the other man had been.

Did he know? Was this a meeting or a fight? She grabbed her winter cloak and ran straight from the room, down the stairs, and out into the night.

* * *

She was still in her boots. Back at Clarfields, she would have been in her satin slippers by now. But Clarfields had carpets and long cushions against the bottoms of the doors to stop draughts. She was glad of the protection on her feet as she raced onto the hard, cold ground at the front of the house.

"Geoffrey?"

A figure came forward from the mist, but it was not Geoffrey. The tall, slender man held his flaming brand aloft, and she recognised his laugh before she recognised his face.

"John Kitt!"

"Good evening, Cordelia, my old friend."

His casualness, his loucheness, once so appealing, now grated. He did it to rile her because he knew she would be riled. She gritted her teeth so that she would not rise to his bait and satisfy his need to make trouble.

But she could think of nothing else to say but "Get away from here!"

He laughed again, and when he brought his free hand forward, his coat flapped out of the way to reveal he held a short, stubby pistol, an old-fashioned looking thing that was as likely to beat you to death as to shoot anything.

She said, "I know you have escaped — you must have — for they have not released you, have they?"

"Of course I escaped," he replied. "You let me, after all."

"I did not! I saw the keys on the ring. Three. You…"

"Oh, you assisted a criminal, all right. You persuaded poor Mrs Revesley to unlock the door, and you saw how she struggled to lock it again, didn't you?"

Realisation dawned. She said, "You had something in the lock to jam it."

"Of course I did. So I suppose I owe you my gratitude and thanks."

Cordelia snorted. "And have you come here this night to thank me? I can assure you, there was no need."

"Well, my gratitude and thanks are not yet enough to save you, your aunt or your household." He crooked his arm and hoisted the pistol in the air and a cold trickle of fear ran down Cordelia's spine.

Where was Geoffrey?

Her fear became an icy ball. Geoffrey had sympathies with this Chartist and his ways. Was he out there, too, ready to turn on her?

No. She would not — could not — believe it. Yes, he had sabotaged the coach. Yes, he ignored her orders. Yes, he was out there, somewhere, with a shotgun.

But no! Not Geoffrey.

She could have cried. But she was Cordelia, Lady Cornbrook and she did not cry — not in front of this pathetic man, at any rate.

"Why would you come after us?" she said, fury and fear thick in her voice. "We are not the mill. My aunt is old, and I am but a visitor here. We have done nothing to you."

"What?" His laugh was indignant. "Yes you have. You are everything that is keeping us down! You are a titled woman. She is of the family that owns near everything around here. You are both symbols, do you not see? Have you learned nothing from my pamphlets, my talks, and my influence on your staff?"

"Your…"

"Yes, my influence. If anything is to change then we must do it from within."

"No," she said. "You are a Chartist and I *have* read your declarations. Suffrage for adult men, and a reform of parliament? Yes. But you cannot do that by filling my servants' heads with rants."

"I think I have left my fellow Chartists behind," he said. "They talk and they talk, but the last petition did not work so why do they think a new one will fare any better? What are names on a piece of paper? The printed word never changed anything."

"The printed word can change the world!"

"I do not see it," he said with scorn. "People do not read words and names but they can read signs, even still, and it is a sign that I shall give them. Things can only really be changed with force. If that were not true, we would have no need for war, would we? But we have war, and this is a war, and so I must use force, and this will send a signal to everything. This is the start. And I am starting with you."

The pistol was lowered. He thrust his hand forward, levelling the fat muzzle towards her.

Time seemed to slow down. Cordelia could not see anything but the misty figure in front of her. The edges of her vision went dark and there was a painful roaring in her ears. She wondered, strangely, if she were about to swoon. Was this what swooning felt like? She had never swooned in her life. Then she wondered why she was thinking about such a stupid thing when she was facing her inevitable death. *What fools we are*, she thought idly. *What fools.*

There was a flash of light, and a bang, as if the light

flared before the sound occurred, and she was momentarily blinded. She staggered back. Had she been hit? Her ears rang, now. *Was this death?* It didn't hurt, if that was the case.

She could hear a bubbling, groaning sound. It wasn't her. She blinked. The muttering and whimpering faded away.

And then a strong man was holding her as her knees collapsed, and she fell against the familiarly horsey smell of her coachman, who let her gently to the ground.

And he muttered, gruffly, "Don't worry, my lady. It's going to be all right. I've shot him."

"Then he will need help…"

"No, my lady. He does not need help now. At this distance, all he needs is a wheelbarrow … to collect the bits."

CHAPTER TWENTY-EIGHT

Cordelia woke late. Her mouth felt furry and her eyes were itchy. She would have claimed that she had not slept a wink — certainly she felt as if she hadn't — but the sunlight in her room proved her wrong. She struggled to sit up.

Ruby was dressed, and watching her. She was half-seated on the low windowsill. "Good morning, my lady."

"Ruby. Ah…"

"No, don't get up. You look like you need rest. I am afraid you've missed church. Your aunt left half an hour ago. I told her you were indisposed."

"What did she say to that?"

"That the best place for someone who was ill was their *own* bed."

"Ouch. Well, indeed. Thank you, Ruby."

Then there was an awkward silence. Cordelia watched

Ruby carefully. Ruby met her gaze unwaveringly.

The previous night … recollections came back to her. John Kitt had been shot. Geoffrey had helped her to the house, and brought her into the hallway. There, he had left her, saying that he had to "attend to the business outside."

Ruby had come out from the kitchen, alerted by the shot. She was holding a warm drink, and had nearly dropped it when she saw Cordelia.

Cordelia assured her that everyone was all right, and was soon in bed, shivering and shaking as she dropped off to sleep. Now she wondered, had Ruby simply stayed alert and wakeful, watching over her all night?

"Ruby, thank you for bringing me to bed last night."

"It is my job, my lady."

Of course. It was her duty. Nothing more? Still, she ought to be grateful for at least that. She said, "Have you seen Geoffrey today?"

"He went into town; I saw him as he left but there was a dark look about him. Darker than usual. My lady … I know we have not been as we once were, lately, but I blame this place. The moors, the weather, it is too desolate here and it puts a shadow on me. But I want to ask … I would have asked … I mean …"

"Last night?"

"Yes, my lady."

"You are perfectly right to ask. You heard … well, no, tell me what you heard."

"A gunshot. I thought it was Maude, again, but then I saw you and I was afraid."

"I see. Ruby, I did not fire a gun. There was an intruder and Geoffrey scared him off. No one was hurt. We are all fine."

"Who was it?"

"A poacher, perhaps? Or another disaffected worker from the mills."

Ruby bit her lip. "Or the murderer. Maybe he has grown bold."

"You do not think that the murderer is John Kitt, then?"

"No," she said, "and nobody does. No, the murderer is still out there. They say, now, that it is a madman who lives on the hills. The newspapers printed a story about a place in Scotland where a man lives in a cave and he snatched young girls from the town and took them back to his cave to be unspeakable with them."

"I am sure that is not the case here," Cordelia said. "Look. We know that Lizzie was obsessed with Percy, but that the love was unrequited. We know that Percy and Iris were lovers. That makes either of them — separately or together — the main suspects. Not some random madman!"

"Well, my lady, you shall never get anyone to agree it could be the Hero of Waterloo and the Great Stoneyford Mill Riot."

"It was hardly a 'great riot'."

"It was the most exciting thing to have happened here — barring the murder — for about half a century."

Cordelia shook her head, but she could feel herself relaxing into a smile. But as soon as she did so, the memory of John Kitt invaded her mind and chilled her all over again. In her imagination he raised a pistol … something fired … and he fell back, and she could hear the sounds. Those awful sounds. The sounds that she now understood to be the sounds of his death.

She had to be sure. She swung her legs out from the bed. "I need to dress for the outdoors," she said. "My warmest walking clothes, please. And then, I shall take a light breakfast in the kitchen — I know, I know, but let them object — before I go out."

* * *

By the time she got to the stables, Geoffrey had returned from his errand to town. He dismissed Stanley, curtly. The pale-faced young man could tell that something had transpired. Maybe he had heard the shot. She wondered what, if anything, Geoffrey had told him. But the coachman sent him to "complete the work on the travelling chariot" and she let him go.

Geoffrey led Cordelia into the tack room. A small lamp gave a little bit of heat and even less light. He offered her a wooden chair but she preferred to stand. It was easier, somehow, to talk about the events in the gloom. She could not see his face very clearly and she hoped that he could not read hers.

"What did you do last night? Was he definitely…"

"Yes, my lady," Geoffrey said in a low rasp. "He was dead. So I took him … it, I ought to say, to town."

"This morning?" she said in horror.

"No," he said, and she could hear a smile tugging at his words. "No, of course not. Last night, I hauled him up into the gig; and he is a heavy man, you know, and I am old. But still fit," he added hastily. "So I managed it, though my back will not be right for a few weeks. I took him to town and all was quiet, and no one saw, I am sure of it. Anyway, I dumped him at the edge. I did not risk driving the gig through the streets."

"And this morning?"

"This morning I went as an innocent man who wanted to buy a pie and a pint of ale. Not being a churchgoer, as you know, this was not so strange…"

"You went for information," she said. "What did you learn?"

"As I thought, they discovered his body, realised he had escaped, found he was shot and dead, and frankly the authorities seem mightily relieved for he saves an awful lot of trouble."

"But they will look into the death, surely?"

"Why? Have they done such a great job of seeking out Lizzie's killer?"

"No."

"Exactly," Geoffrey said. "For them, he was trouble, and now that trouble is gone. He was a Chartist, once, but he became more, or less, perhaps, than he should have been."

Cordelia asked, carefully, "So you do not agree with his principles?"

"I agree with his principles, most definitely, my lady," he said vehemently. "But I do not necessarily agree with his methods, that is all."

"Yet you still work for me," she said.

"As a free man. I could leave at any time."

"But you won't."

"I won't. But this goes two ways."

And she saw that she could not leave him behind again, and she smiled. "We cannot talk of this again," she said. "What does Stanley know?"

"Nothing. And Ruby?"

"Nothing."

"Good," he said. "Soon we must go home."

"I know, and we are ready to travel tomorrow or the next day at the very latest. Christmas looms within the week. And it is not a short journey home; we will make as few overnight stops as possible, but even so, I don't imagine we will be home before Christmas Eve."

"So much for your plans."

"Indeed," she said.

"You are still reluctant to leave?" he said, catching the hesitation in her voice. "I think Mrs Unsworth is fretting for you to come back to Clarfields."

"I know. Yet I am reluctant, yes. I worry for my aunt, though she cannot wait for us to go. And Lizzie preys on my mind. I told Ruby I'd find the killer. I am letting you all down…"

"We will find the killer," Geoffrey said.

"You don't think it was Kitt, either?"

"No," he said. "But look to Captain Percy Slatters."

"I intend to," she said. "He is hiding something."

"I think," Geoffrey said, "he is hiding himself."

CHAPTER TWENTY-NINE

Maude was sniffy with Cordelia when she returned from church, and the sniffiness quickly devolved into straight-out acrimony when Maude told Cordelia about her expected visitors. She was still set upon the séance, and Cordelia would have nothing to do with it.

"How can you do this after being at church, in the house of God, this morning?" Cordelia asked as they drank a cup of tea together after the midday meal.

"I did not see *you* there," Maude replied. "I rarely socialise, but as it is the festive season, why should I not have my friends to visit?"

"I applaud that and totally agree with you, dear aunt. But a séance? Really?"

"Why not? It is just a bit of fun."

"I see you in a new and different light," Cordelia said. "I do not think this is appropriate. I assumed you would be the last person to condone such things."

"You cannot tell me what is, and is not, appropriate. Why the objection?"

Cordelia played with her cup. "I feel uncomfortable with it. It's messing with things that we ought not mess with. Spirits, maybe. Or just people's minds. I don't know. What would the Reverend say?"

"I don't know; I can never hear him."

"It seems unchristian."

"It depends on one's idea of that."

Cordelia shook her head. "No, aunt, I cannot be a part of this. I would feel duplicitous."

"Suit yourself. Are you leaving today?"

"Tomorrow … or Tuesday."

"Good."

* * *

Cordelia went into town that afternoon. Shops were open again, so that the workers could buy what they needed for the week ahead. She took Ruby, and they rode in the travelling chariot. The large carriage struggled at first but the road improved as they neared the town, and Stanley was a careful and competent driver — whatever Geoffrey might insinuate.

"Iris would have loved the séance," Ruby said. "Me, I don't get it, all that stuff."

"Nor do I, but it troubles me," Cordelia said. "My aunt is inconsistent."

"People are, my lady!" Ruby said with a laugh. "That's half the point of being people. You can't just write out a list of the traits of a person's personality and expect them to always be like that."

"No, I suppose not. But how messy!"

Ruby grinned.

It was much more pleasant to be in the enclosed carriage with their feet on hot bricks as they nestled back amongst cushions. It was a rocky bumpy ride, but at least they were away from the elements.

The carriage drew to a halt and they dashed through the icy air to the sanctity of the inn. Cordelia had dressed in drab colours, and with Ruby next to her, she hoped she did not stand out. The maid offered them a private room, but when Cordelia refused, she just shrugged and waved them into the cosy and slightly more refined saloon lounge. It was about as low as Cordelia was going to able to sink; she peered through the door to the public bar but with its bare floor and raucous crowds, it did not appeal in the broad light of day, even if she could have entered.

And even that was not as low as the beer houses that were springing up since the Act of 1830. To "reduce public drunkenness" — particularly the imbibing of gin — the government had relaxed the rules on purchasing beer. Workers on low wages would be there, not here in the coaching inn.

Cordelia took a table that was enclosed by high-backed settles, and Ruby brought her drink and cushions. They sipped at their watered wine and watched the people around them.

It was for word of John Kitt that Cordelia was here. She was gripped by waves of nauseating fear that she and Geoffrey would be discovered as the killers; and that Kitt's escape would be traced to her. Surely they would have spoken to Mrs Revesley!

"What did you hear when you went to buy the wine?" she asked in a low voice.

Ruby leaned forward, and slid her eyes sideways while she replied, keeping her gaze on the mass of people. "Nothing," she said. "No one is speaking of Kitt. Percy Slatters is here, you know; just beyond that knot of men that would be bankers if they had had a wash."

Cordelia could see four men in black, with braying laughs. They were mostly older men, who should have been at home with their families on a Sunday afternoon. They were probably clerks and minor business-folk who had never made it in the cities. And just past them, yes, she could see the sandy mop of Percy's head.

"So he's still the hero of the hour, is he?" she said.

"In here he is, my lady. Amongst these people, yes. I should think he does not get the same reception in the public bar."

"Indeed not." For there, he would be drinking with the men he had charged with his cavalry, and mothers of the children he had injured.

Both John Kitt and Geoffrey had mentioned Percy and she herself had nagging doubts. But one could not accuse a man of murder based on a nagging doubt. Was there evidence that he needed to get rid of Lizzie? Had he lain with her, and was she with child?

"Ruby, do you think that Lizzie could have been pregnant?"

Ruby clapped a hand over her mouth. Muffled, and with snorts of laughter, she said, "My lady, no. She was intent on marriage, and nothing would have persuaded her to … have a trial run. I did not know her well, but I know that."

"Even with alcohol? And … force?"

"No, my lady, I don't believe that. She gave no sign, in word or deed."

"Huh." Cordelia rested her chin on her hands. "But there is something not right about that captain. Captain … captain." Then she sat bold upright. "Waterloo was an awfully long time ago."

Ruby flicked off the years on her fingers. "Thirty years, my lady."

"Let me think back. He told me he was there as a boy … a general soldier … no, that cannot be. For his commission will have been purchased … could he have … I mean, I know nothing of the way the ranks work, but you cannot go from being a rank and file soldier to being an officer, can you?"

Ruby pursed her lips. "You know, you are right, I think. You are one or the other. An officer is a gentleman with money. A common soldier is … a blunt instrument, a weapon himself really. And of a different class altogether."

"So if he was a nothing, a common soldier at Waterloo, he would not be an officer now — even if he could have bought his commission."

"Unlikely," Ruby said. "But who knows? If a really able soldier shows promise, and commitment, and can pay—"

"All those things will not change the class he was born into."

"Until he gets the vote."

"Hush, now, you Chartist. So, either he lied about being at Waterloo, or he…"

"…or he is not an officer now," Ruby finished for her.

"It is far more likely that he has lied about being at

Waterloo," Cordelia said.

"Is it? Why would he lie about that?"

"To gain admiration."

Ruby huffed. "No. There are other battles he could have named. More recent ones."

"Yes, but more recent ones run the risk of him meeting someone who *was* there and being called out for it."

"So, what are we saying?" Ruby said. "That he definitely is an officer, but has lied about his service record? Because there is another thing about this man: he is old for the army."

"There is some duplicity at work here," Cordelia said. "Some lie or subterfuge. Let us peep beyond the veil, Ruby…"

"What do you mean?"

Cordelia knocked back the last of her slightly bitter wine, and thumped the table. "Let us talk to him. You must watch his face, and watch his movements for any betrayal. His body will give us a sign when we are close to the truth."

"Ha, like Maude's spirits rapping on a table."

"Just so. Come on."

Ruby followed Cordelia past the shabby businessmen. Percy looked up and greeted them with a wide grin, his face shiny with heat and alcohol.

"Dear lady, you are mingling with the wrong sort," he

said, bowing low and reaching for her hand.

She kept her hand at her side. "Do not fear; I shall not talk with you long."

"I did not mean me — but, ah, you are of course correct." He straightened up. "Allow me to purchase you a drink."

"No, thank you," Cordelia said, and Ruby tutted. Cordelia elbowed her maid discretely. "You mentioned, when we first met, that you had been at Waterloo and that was what inspired you to dedicate your life to military service…"

"Indeed, my lady!"

"Right. And you were…?"

He hesitated. "A drummer boy."

"A boy?"

"I was fifteen, my lady. It was no place for a callow youth but I grew up very fast. But this is not talk for a Sunday afternoon; this is the time for merriment and friends. Let us drink!"

"And now you are an officer," she said. "Were the Hussars at Waterloo?"

"One does not have to remain with the same regiment," he said, and his fingers were twitching. He smiled thinly. "Ah, my lady, the military world is a strange one. Confusing, even to those within it! Do not try to understand it from outside. The rules, the rituals, the traditions…"

"Such as the tradition of purchasing a commission?"

"Naturally."

"So you are from a well-bred family?"

"They are all long dead, I am afraid. But not a day goes by when I do not mourn them! And, speaking of families, how is your wonderful aunt? And the mill? I trust that no more trouble has beset them…"

She knew he was angling for a compliment for his fine deeds. She ignored it. "And when did you take up your commission?" she asked. She stood casually, trying to look relaxed and merely idly curious, nothing more.

But suspicions had been raised — and not just with Percy himself. The stale odour of Constable Kennett drifted closer. He had been listening. "This does seem like a rum old do, as it were," he said. "I, as for me myself, why yes, I should be very interested in finding out more. Do tell us, Captain, and put us out of our misery."

Percy's eyes were bulging and his face was tight around his lips. He said, "Oh for — for goodness sake! What of a man's past? The only thing we can ever be sure of is this moment, right now. Let us drink to good friends, a bright future and the safety of the mill! Hooray!"

"You prevaricate, so you do, sir," Kennett said. He

might not have been the brightest button but it was now obvious to all that Percy did not want to talk about his past, and even a drink-dulled constable knew that this was something to pursue. "Simply give me some dates, that is all; indeed, simply explain how you began as a drummer boy, as you claim, and ended up an officer, as you are now. For that is an unusual story, and I am sure we would all love to be inspired by such a meteoric rise in fortunes."

Percy drew himself up very straight. There was fury in his expression, and something else, too. Fear? Or calculation? It was hard to tell. He took a deep breath and said in an unexpectedly low voice, "I am sorry to disappoint you all but the tale will have to wait for another day. I can see one of my men outside, and he is signalling to me; I will return as soon as I know what he wants me for." He had affected his 'I am an officer and you will listen to me' voice and he took two brisk steps in the direction of the door.

But one of the businessmen, all of whom had been avidly listening, said, "There is no one out there. I can see through the windows."

"He has gone to the door—"

"What utter nonsense," Kennett said, and Cordelia was glad she had given the man a pie because now he earned it by grabbing Percy's arm.

Percy wrenched himself free but the inn's patrons

closed around him. Kennett began to inform him that he was being arrested, and his voice had to rise louder and louder over Percy's protests. Then Kennett grabbed him again, and the businessman who had spoken up came forward to assist. Percy kicked out, and caught Kennett on the shin.

"And now I shall have to add 'assault' to the list," the constable said.

"The list of what?" Percy said desperately as he was dragged towards the door. "You have not made it plain what I am being arrested for."

"You are lying about something, that much is obvious. And now you are resisting arrest, and you have assaulted me. This is all rather interesting."

"Where are we going? Not the pig sty—"

"No, sir, not for you. If you are, indeed, an officer, then it is only right that we lock you up somewhere here — gentlemen, let us take him upstairs to a room that might be made fast, and then I shall report all to the Justice."

"No!"

And then they were gone, and Ruby was looking at Cordelia with a smile but lowered brows. "You should have accepted his offer of a drink before he was arrested," was all she said.

CHAPTER THIRTY

Cordelia avoided Maude on Sunday evening. One of Maude's friends had remained after the séance and joined them for dinner, but Cordelia made the minimum of polite conversation before excusing herself before the dessert course came.

Back in their rooms, Ruby was packing. Cordelia stood at the door and watched the maid crumple her clothing into the chest with no thought or care.

"You don't want to go, do you?" Cordelia said.

"I do, and I don't. Everything feels pointless."

"On the contrary, I think we are close to discovering all there is to know about Percy Slatters and I think he is linked to Lizzie McNab."

"The murderer? Yes. The more I know about him, my lady, the more I think he could have done it, now."

"Tomorrow we will go to talk to him and to Iris once

more. I have some questions."

"Shall I still pack?"

"If you don't," Cordelia said, "I rather fear my aunt will come in here and pack for us. So yes, continue as you are please. But ... do fold the clothes."

* * *

Constable Kennett still looked at her like she could be unwrapped like a parcel just for him, but he spoke with respect when she greeted him on Monday morning at the inn. He was pleased that she had led him to Percy and had given him a reason to arrest and investigate the "hero of the mill." He told her that he had always been suspicious of Percy. She knew that if she had not begun the unmasking so publicly, Kennett would have been taking the credit, too.

"They are both securely locked up," he assured her. "I am going to fetch some breakfast now, as I cannot work on an empty stomach, you know. It is fuel for the brain. Did you know that oats can strengthen a man's heart? It is why the Scots are so hale and hearty et cetera. But yes, go on up and see what else your so-charming feminine wiles can wheedle out of him. Or her, even, of course, ha ha."

"Ha. Ha. Quite." She gave him enough of a smile to make him feel warm, and headed up the stairs to the bare corridor.

She went first to speak to Iris. She felt sure she could

unbolt the door and join the young woman, and she was right; the seamstress wasn't about to pull any of the tricks that John Kitt had tried. Iris was sitting on her bed, staring at the Bible that rested, unopened, in her hands. The room did not smell fresh, and Iris was looking pale and careworn. Her hair was neatly done, but it needed a good wash. She looked up with hard, red-rimmed eyes.

"My lady."

"Good morning, Iris." Cordelia sat on the far end of the bed. "So, have you heard the latest news?"

"John Kitt is dead, and good riddance to him. He shall have no peace."

"Ah — no, I did not mean that. I meant that your lover, Percy Slatters, is held here as a prisoner also."

She lifted one shoulder in a tiny shrug. "Oh, yes, they told me that, too."

Iris's complete lack of concern was interesting. "Are you not troubled at all?"

"He is nothing to me, nothing," Iris said, and at last a hint of emotion came into her otherwise dull voice. "He is a liar, as you have all found out."

"What is he lying about? That he was at Waterloo?"

"Oh, he was there. But he is no officer. I am amazed that he has fooled you all so long. But then, he fooled me also. The spirits allowed it. They wanted to teach me a lesson, I suppose."

"How, then is he here, leading the Yeomanry?"

"That is easy, my lady. He met the real captain riding on the road to come here and take up his position. And you can imagine what happened next."

"Goodness me. Have you evidence of this?"

Iris twisted her head and looked directly at Cordelia. "No."

She looked away, dropped her gaze, and a tear plopped onto her hand. She whispered again, "no," but Cordelia was not sure that it was addressed to her at all. She quietly withdrew.

* * *

Cordelia went straight down the corridor to Percy's room, but here she knew not to take the risk and unlock the door. She knocked, and called out softly, with her head close to the frame. "Captain Percy Slatters?"

"Hello? Who is that? Lady Cornbrook?"

"Yes. I was wondering how you fared today."

There was a silence for a minute and she thought he was going to refuse to respond. After all, it was her fault, in effect, that he was now incarcerated.

But he relented. Curiosity probably got the better of him. "Well, I have been in nicer situations," he said. "What do you want, exactly? Are you come to let me out? Why don't you step within, if you want to talk…"

"I think not," she said. "Thank you anyway. So, this is an interesting situation; you are here, and your lover Iris is just down the corridor."

"My lover?"

"Yes. Do you deny it?"

There was a pained silence. Eventually he said, quietly, "How is she?"

Cordelia considered that an admission. "Have you not spoken to her?"

"I have shouted but I fear she does not hear me."

"She might be ignoring you. I have just spoken with her, and she is not terribly keen on you at the moment."

He made a spluttering sound. "Oh, tish. She does have her moods, does our Iris. Now, about this mix-up. I don't know why everyone has suddenly got it in for me. Really, I can only suppose that with that vile troublemaker Kitt out of the way, people around here want a new villain to hate. But they've got me all wrong. You know the Justice, Mr Gold, don't you? I am sure you can explain the issue…"

"But that's the thing. I don't know what the issue is, because you have not explained anything."

Surely he could have come up with a half-decent explanation overnight, she thought. She waited, but nothing was forthcoming. He simply said, "There has been a mistake, and if I were allowed to get to my barracks, I could produce all the evidence that anyone would wish for. Perhaps you would be so kind as to…"

"No."

She sought a way to get him to open up. She wanted to ask a clever question that would trip him up. But forcing her brain to work faster seemed to slow it down. There was certainly something off-kilter between him and Iris, though. She said, stalling for time, "My aunt held a séance yesterday, you know. Your Iris would have loved that."

He laughed. "Indeed she would, and I also."

"You? I am surprised."

"Oh, I don't believe any of that stuff — who does? But the gullible are a treat to watch and to — well, they get what they deserve, do they not? You seem to me to be an uncommonly rational woman. How did you find the event?"

"I did not attend. Thank you, and good-day."

"Wait, is that it?"

She turned back to the door. "Have you more to say?"

"No. It's just that … well, I rather expected you to pump me for more information."

"Do you have more information you would share?"

"Well, no."

"It is just a game, and it is one I choose not to play with you. Goodbye."

She walked briskly back to Four Trees. She had said the right things, but more by accident than design; still, she had a clearer idea now, of the answer. He had given himself away.

She did not yet have all the pieces that made the solution work, however.

CHAPTER THIRTY-ONE

"Come on, you."

Maude spoke brusquely and Cordelia was surprised. No sooner had she entered the manor house, than her aunt was pulling her back towards the door again.

"Dear aunt! I promise I shall leave tomorrow at the latest! Are you throwing me out onto the street?"

"No," Maude said, her bony fingers digging into Cordelia's arm. "We are going to spend the afternoon making calls. Well, one call. And that call is to Mr William Gold's house. He has said he is at home today and I thought you could talk with him, wrap everything up that is obsessing you so inappropriately, and there, be done with it. I know you cannot go until you have answers. So, let us go and fetch those answers. Into the carriage with you!"

* * *

The visit began badly.

"Did you know?" Cordelia hissed, pulling her aunt backwards. The old lady tottered and nearly fell, and Cordelia cursed herself. But rage was tingling in her fingers. She steadied Maude, but did not relent as she dragged her behind some heavy burgundy curtains that screened off an alcove around a recessed window in William Gold's large receiving room.

"Did you know that *he* was going to be here?" she persisted.

Maude blew out her cheeks and worked her thin lips. Her eyes were large and she said, "No, and I am so very sorry."

That stopped Cordelia short. An apology? The rare admission from the otherwise rock-hard woman proved her truth. Cordelia sighed. "So what do we do now?"

"We can simply leave," Maude said. "We have been here fifteen minutes, which is long enough to be polite."

"I haven't spoken to Mr Gold himself yet!" Since their arrival, Mr Gold had greeted them and made them comfortable but had had to excuse himself to finish a conversation with another visitor, and that formality concluded, he had been waylaid by a strident woman on his way to talk to Cordelia. He had telegraphed his apology through upraised eyebrows, and she had smiled, and turned, and seen — like a blow to the heart — Hugo Hawke saunter into the room.

It seemed that the Justice didn't often receive callers because this "at-home" afternoon had attracted every half-decent local person of standing within a ten mile radius.

But Hugo Hawke was well out of that radius. He had a large estate in Cambridgeshire. He had been Cordelia's late husband's friend, and trustee of his estates, preventing Cordelia from inheriting any land — until she had won her home back in a bet. She'd refused his offer of marriage and left in a hurry.

"I will feign an illness," Maude said. "I am old, and can do these things."

Cordelia suddenly felt a strong family tie to Maude. That was exactly the sort of ruse that Cordelia herself would want to try. "Thank you, dear aunt. I think it will be our only chance. It is a shame I have not spoken to Mr Gold, though."

"What were you going to say, exactly?"

"I wanted to talk to him about certain things I have discovered regarding both Percy Slatters and Iris Fletcher."

Maude shuddered. "Terrible people, both. I wish life did not have these tedious complications."

"I know, and I appreciate your forbearance in this matter."

"My forbearance is running out, hence our visit here.

However, I understand why you cannot stay."

"Thank you."

Maude thinned her lips but her expression was resigned. "I want nothing more than peace and quiet as I shuffle towards my death, alone. And here you are, poking and prying. But if I were you … yes, I would be doing the same."

Cordelia saw, then, that her own vitality was a constant kick in the teeth to Maude. She was about to say something conciliatory, but Maude went on. "Anyway. Let us be honest, and this will hurt you, but I suspect you already know this: what will Mr Gold do with your knowledge, your discoveries, do you think?"

Cordelia peeped around the curtain and surveyed the hot, busy room. "Nothing," she muttered. "Yet I felt sure I could make him see sense if I laid all the facts out…"

"He is not expecting to hear facts from you, and that, I have found, is the biggest obstacle. People hear what they expect."

"Then how can I get justice for Lizzie?"

"You can't," Maude said.

"Then why did you bring me here?" She felt suddenly as if she had been played with.

"So you could talk to him at least, get it off your chest, do as much as you possibly can, and then you will be able to go home with an easier conscience."

"But—" Cordelia felt her shoulders sag. She could not, not with Hugo Hawke there. She had to leave before he saw her.

Maude patted her arm. "You can only do as much as you can do, and no more. The fault, then, is not with you at all, is it?"

"I suppose not."

"Shall we go?"

"I suppose so."

"Will you talk to Mr Gold?"

Cordelia shook her head. "You know there is no point. I know there is no point, either, but I have been too stubborn to accept defeat."

Maude smiled then. "I know. And I am proud of you, you know." She lifted her chin and assumed a serious face again. "Now, let us get away from here. You go to the door and make good your escape; I shall run the gauntlet. I can do a convincing poor-old-lady act for Mr Gold, and I shall meet you in the carriage."

But it was not to be. Cordelia stepped out from the curtain and Maude came behind her, but before they could peel off to their respective destinations, Hugo caught sight of Cordelia from across the room.

Usually she liked her imposing height, but it did make

it difficult to creep through a room unseen. Maude came in front of Cordelia but it was like a Dachshund masking a Great Dane.

"Oho, so the rumour was true; here you are, Lady Cornbrook." He did not bow and he did not take her hand. His shocking lack of proper formality made it very clear to her — and anyone watching — the scant regard he held for her.

"Mr Hawke," she said. "Do excuse us. We were just leaving."

Maude stepped up to the challenge and in a tiny, trembling voice, she said, "I am unwell and I have ruined my dear niece's visit but alas, that is the trial of being old…"

Hugo rolled his eyes. "You two are related? Then I believe none of it. You are simply avoiding me."

Maude gasped. Even if he did not believe her, he should have pretended to. Cordelia narrowed her eyes. "Come away, Aunt. Do not let him goad you."

William Gold was now upon them, and he was smiling broadly. "So you are all already acquainted? How marvellous! Dear Lady Cornbrook, I do apologise for neglecting you earlier. Now, come, tell me all about your house and estate."

In light of the history of the house and its acrimonious associations between her and Hugo, that was exactly the wrong thing to say.

"And has this woman told you how she acquired that house?" Hugo said.

"Oh, is it an interesting tale?" Mr Gold said, distracted by Hugo's dangerous smile.

"It is not," Cordelia said at the same time as her aunt said, "Dear William, I am afraid I must retire…"

"And what are you meddling with up here?" Hugo said, his eyes meeting Cordelia's.

"I am merely visiting my aunt."

"Unlikely."

"It is true!"

Mr Gold laughed, but a little nervously this time, as he began to perceive the undercurrents in the shark-infested conversation. "She has been rather drawn to the recent unfortunate events of this locality but I suppose that a clever woman will be curious about all matters. It seems to be a growing trend, you know. A lady of my acquaintance takes all the London papers, and has done since she was fourteen. Yes! It is the truth."

"The unfortunate events? Oh, some slattern was found dead, was she not?" Hugo said. "Oh, really, Lady Cornbrook — you think your lucky strike in Cambridgeshire somehow qualifies you to take up detectoring?"

"Is this a habit of yours, Lady Cornbrook?" Mr Gold asked.

"No, not at all. But, like all decent citizens, I strive for justice and wish only to see the evil doers punished."

Hugo brayed a laugh. He turned to the Justice of the Peace. "Now, tell me, Sir, has she been asking questions and meddling and coming up with wild fancies? Has she been mixing with all manner of people, blithely disregarding all social norms? She is quite the eccentric, you know."

"She has," Mr Gold said slowly. "But I must defend the lady, as she is quite correct in wishing for criminals to be found out."

"Defend? Ha! People will talk, you know. She is not welcome in most proper parlours. Not at all. Let me advise you; do not let her taint bring scandal to your door."

"Now see here!" Maude had lost her little-old-lady voice. "You will *not* speak of my family in that manner."

"Dear Miss Stanbury, I am sure my *guest* Mr Hawke has no intention of *slandering you.*" Mr Gold spoke warningly, and Hugo simmered down, a little flushed.

"Thank you so much for your hospitality," Cordelia said, making a supreme effort to sound light and breezy. "I am afraid we must go."

Hugo opened his mouth, and found himself on the receiving end of glares from Mr Gold, Maude and Cordelia herself. He chose politeness, and pressed his lips together.

He could not, however, resist a final parting jibe as Cordelia and Maude reached the door. A liveried servant swung the double doors open and as they stepped through, Hugo said, "Give it up, Lady Cornbrook. You are a laughing stock. Find a husband — if there is still a man out there who will accept you — and give up solving crimes."

She whirled around. "I shall not. I will solve this one, too, just you see."

Even Mr Gold had to laugh at that. "Dear Lady Cornbrook…"

"I nearly have it, you know," she said, defiantly. "I have the answer. I do not yet have the pieces but I am close."

Maude hissed, "Come away. I have to live here amongst these people!"

Cordelia scanned the room. People looked away rather than meet her eyes. *So be it,* she thought, and followed Maude out to the carriage.

CHAPTER THIRTY-TWO

She had it.

She *had* it.

She was so close. Cordelia retreated to her room in silence that night. She assured her aunt she would be gone on Tuesday; she could leave it no later. She sat by the fire, ignoring Ruby, focusing deep within herself. She cast herself back and re-imagined every conversation she had had with all of the principle players. She recalled every conversation, every twitch, and at each point she asked herself: *what did that person want?* Unravelling their desires was the key to their actions.

On Tuesday morning she left Geoffrey and Ruby packing the travelling chariot. She got Stanley to drive her in the gig back to the inn. It was bitterly cold and they were both wrapped up like Russians.

The newspaper man was back in the lobby of the inn.

When he saw her, he laughed. "Ah! Good morning, Lady Cornbrook."

"You're the man from the Gazette."

"I am. And I know who you are, now. I reckon I have a nose for ferreting out the truth, in the end. No sign of this terrifying husband. Eh?"

"You have unmasked me. Well done. What are you doing here?"

"Two people are upstairs, both under lock and key! There is a story here, you know."

"There is that. I rather think that you might be useful. What's your name, fellow?"

He bowed low. "Gerald Templeton, at your service."

"Mr Templeton, would you care to accompany me upstairs?"

A flicker of suspicion crossed his face. "Undoubtedly I would, but I have also heard about your prowess with a barometer."

"Oh, don't worry, that was simply my maid. High spirits, bless her."

"In that case, madam, lead on."

* * *

Cordelia stood halfway down the corridor. Iris's room was to her right and Percy was locked up on her left. She called out in a strident and unwomanly voice, "Captain

Percy Slatters?"

"Is that Lady Cornbrook? Good morning," he called back.

"Iris Fletcher? Can you hear me?"

There was no reply to that, but Cordelia was sure that Iris could hear her very well through the thin wooden doors.

John Kitt talked of duplicity. She had thought he meant Percy, and his lies. The man was no captain; he was a fake and charlatan.

But perhaps Kitt had meant Iris, not Percy. Iris, with her spirits and her visions. "Iris Fletcher, the dead talk to you, do they not?"

"They do." Iris's voice was low but surprisingly near; she was standing quite close behind her door, Cordelia realised.

"There are those who make a living from talking with the dead, and passing messages on," Cordelia said. "One such came to my aunt's séance a few days ago, apparently."

"Those people are liars," Iris said. She raised her voice. "Liars!"

Percy heard that, and Iris must have meant him to. "Iris, listen, sweetheart. We had a future together. We can get out of this, you and I."

"Percy, I know you are no captain," Cordelia said.

"My commission — well, let me explain. Er…"

"Oh, save it. You met the real captain on the road here, and took his place."

"I did not kill him!" Percy blurted out. The newspaper man was writing as quickly as his fingers would allow. "No, of course, I... oh."

"So there proves your guilt," Cordelia said. "At least in your fakery."

There was a low thud against the door. He may have struck it in frustration, or simply let his head bang upon it. Percy said, "Well, then. Yes, so you have found me out. I assume he is still alive. I did not bump his head hard enough to kill."

"But he has not followed you here, so..."

"Ah. Yes. Well, I tell myself that many things may have befallen him..."

"No, Percy," she said. "If this man that you robbed has not pursued you here, you must face the truth."

"I am not a killer," he said, his voice weak, and she believed him; he was not an intentional killer. But the fact that the real captain had not raised the alarm was proof, to her mind, that he had not survived the robbery.

"How did you think you would get away with it?" she asked.

"I was not intending to stay very long. But then I met Iris."

"Not Lizzie?"

"Oh, she was … not for me. She thought I was real. But Iris, now Iris, she is a woman of my heart. She understands me."

"I am sorry to say that I rather fear she did not understand you — until it was too late. And you do not understand her, at all."

"In that she is a woman—"

"No," Cordelia said. "In that she is in earnest when she speaks of spirits."

"No, no," he said, almost laughing in a desperate and manic way. "No, it is all nonsense. We were to … we were to …"

"Go on. You can hardly get yourself in more trouble, can you? You have as good as admitted to killing the real captain of the Hussars."

They waited, the newspaper man's pencil poised until Percy finally spoke. "Iris and me, we are two halves of a whole. I know she is quiet and reserved, but she has her own secrets, her own past that—"

"Percy, no!" Iris shouted.

"—that I will let her relate. But suffice it to say that together, we planned to travel and to perform, and to conjure spirits and to relieve the rich of their money via their incredulity, if you see what I mean."

"You and Iris?" Cordelia said. "What, travelling together and putting on shows? As mediums, is that what you are saying?"

"Oh, not real ones, of course," Percy said.

"You are a traitor and a liar!" Iris called. "My spirits are real. I thought that Percy was real but all along, he was a liar ... a fake ... wanting to use my gifts for money."

"No, Iris, no! Come on now; your 'gifts' are very handy but they are not real, are they?"

"Yes!"

Cordelia stepped in. She said, "And there is the problem, as you can surely see it, Mr Templeton."

The newspaper man nodded, his face alight with the story of betrayal and misunderstanding. "Indeed, my lady! Here we have a chancer of a man, someone who travels and takes on new identities like changing a hat, and he falls in with this woman who believes herself to have a true gift. But so blinded is he by love, he cannot see her faith; and I suppose she, too, was blinded by love?"

"At least at the beginning," Cordelia said. "I think Iris thought that Percy did believe her. But what I do not understand, Iris Fletcher, is why you would have been attracted to a man like this in the first place? You are an honest, decent hard working woman ... aren't you?"

Silence.

Duplicity, thought Cordelia. John Kitt knew. *How did he know?* "Iris," Cordelia said, "You have told me a little of your past. Why not tell us again, for the benefit of this newspaper man I have here, so that he might set your story straight?"

"Indeed," Mr Templeton said in an encouraging tone, sidling closer to the locked door. "Here is your chance to get in first! Let me tell the world your truth."

"No."

Cordelia said, "Iris, you are not what you seem." She probed at the idea of the relationship between Percy and Iris. What had he seen in her, to make him think they would work so well together? "You travel as a seamstress. This is a loose and rootless existence. You slip from place to place … you're welcomed into houses, but you do not stay long. You avoid people. You…" She remembered, then, a threat from before. The threat of having stolen goods placed in one's belongings, the threat of an accusation — how unfair!

How unfair if *untrue*.

"You use this transient lifestyle, do you not?" Cordelia said.

Still silence.

The girl was clever and she was stubborn. Cordelia wanted to wheedle a confession out of her, but how? She had nothing to bargain with.

Or maybe she did. "Tell me about Lizzie McNab," Cordelia said. "Iris, you knew her. You shared a room with her."

"I've told you everything."

"No," Cordelia said. "You haven't told us how you killed her."

When the silence rolled back in this time, it was thin and strained, as if everyone was waiting for someone else to speak first. Cordelia went back over it in her head; yes, it was clear to her now. Iris's lack of denial or lack of confirmation was neither here nor there.

It was Percy who broke. "No, not Iris. No! You're all wrong, Lady Cornbrook. Why would she? How could she?"

"If Iris can tell us her background, then the newspaper can print it and the jury might be swayed by her tale of woe; I am sure that a young woman like Iris has been subject to a hard past which might go some way, perhaps, to explaining her recent actions..." Cordelia tailed off. She sounded fake and false even to her own ears, but it was worth a try.

Iris was not for biting. "There won't be a jury," she said. "I am innocent of everything but loving a stupid man. Soon they will have to release me. John Kitt killed Lizzie; Percy is a fake; and I am wrongly imprisoned. There, that is your story."

320

"Iris!" Percy called, his voice plaintive. Then it changed, taking on a harder note. "Iris, I have always defended you…"

This was their way in, Cordelia saw. She did not speak, but when she made eye contact with Mr Templeton, he nodded, and moved towards Percy's door. He, too, could now see where the final pieces of the puzzle would come from.

"She did not kill anyone, I am sure of it," Percy said. "You said there is a newspaper man out there with you? Then ensure you write this down, sir. She did not kill anyone. But you're correct, Lady Cornbrook, in that poor Miss Fletcher has had a hard time of things. Yes, she may have been forced to act in some … unbecoming … ways, but don't we all, to survive? That Kitt fellow, he had some good ideas, you know. We can't all go on staying poor and being grateful for that poverty, you know?"

"Tell us about Iris's 'hard time' as you call it," Cordelia said.

"NO!"

Percy ignored the seamstress's cry. "Only this: that she has been cruelly served by fate. She lost her apprenticeship and was cast out, you know, through no fault of her own. Then her family disappeared, and she was lost, alone, quite friendless and without a penny to her name. What would you do?"

"I know not."

"Well, she is resourceful and she knew she had to set up as a seamstress to use her skills. For that, she needed money."

"Percy!"

"So she collected money as a charity—"

"No!"

"But I see little wrong with this," Percy blithely continued. "She was in need of charity herself, and who would have begrudged her a coin or two?"

"But for which charity did she collect?" Mr Templeton asked.

"Oh, ah, sick children or some such, I believe. People can't resist a poorly babe."

"And so she is a fraudster, just like you," Cordelia said.

Percy was on a roll now. "Oh, she is cleverer than I! We met in an inn, you know; she had ordered food and said she was waiting for her husband who would pay. Of course he never did…"

"Goodness," Cordelia said. "I had not expected that."

"There is more. In the houses that she stayed in…"

"Percy! You coward, you cad, you must stop!"

He did. But he had said enough, and Cordelia could fill in the blanks. "She would steal, would she not? It is a common and sordid tale."

Now they could hear low sobbing from the other room. "You have ruined me, Percy," she said.

"No, Iris, you are innocent and we will leave and—"

"Never, not with you! Now they will look at me and see a cheat and they will poke and pry until…"

"Until?" Cordelia said. "Until we know the truth?"

More sobbing, and in amongst the plaintive wails, Cordelia heard her say, "But it was her destiny to die."

Mr Templeton's pencil was flying.

CHAPTER THIRTY-THREE

No more sense could be got from Iris, but Mr Templeton said to Cordelia, "My lady, this certainly warrants further investigation. If you will take a room here for an hour or so, I shall send food and drink; you can wait while I engage the Justice to come out."

She willingly conceded.

While she waited, she went over it in her mind. Iris had killed Lizzie. She formulated the method — it must have been opium, to start. Had she intended to kill her? *Yes,* Cordelia decided, because as well as the traces of drug, Lizzie had also shown signs of suffocation. Therefore Lizzie must have started to come around, and Iris had finished the deed, possibly in a state of panic.

Lizzie would have been lured to the Ally Cross either by the promise of meeting Percy, or simply by Iris offering to take a walk with her; that was not so unthinkable.

And why did Iris have to kill Lizzie?

That was almost too simple. It was jealousy. Lizzie loved Percy and cleaved to him; Iris could not stand it. She had to get Lizzie out of the way. Percy probably loved the attention. And Iris was worried about Lizzie influencing Percy. And perhaps she also knew too much about Iris, about her past, and about her light-fingered tendencies.

Ultimately, Iris was a sad, lonely, and troubled young woman and she had fallen under Percy's spell; the spell which had been broken too late. Percy had charmed her, and Iris had been ready for the charming, and had not seen that Percy did not believe, as she did, in the spirits.

Cordelia felt a desperate sympathy for the seamstress. That feeling did not prevent her from laying all her thoughts bare to Mr Gold when he arrived. He harrumphed and blustered, but he listened to her carefully.

"I shall say that I suspect you might be correct, my lady," he said at the end. "But we need evidence, and if we have that as a confession from her own mouth, so much the better."

"Present all these facts to her most baldly," Cordelia advised. "Tell her, plainly, that she is found out; and she will cave. She believes in destiny and she will just take this as the next part of the universe's plan for her."

"Do you think so?"

"I am very sure of it," Cordelia said. "I have begun to understand this woman's mind, I think. Such as it is."

"Well, I shall defer to your feminine knowledge," he said. "Where do you go now?"

"I will return to my aunt's house but we do not tarry long; I intend to be on the road by nightfall."

"Then only let me have your address and I shall be sure to send word of the outcomes."

She appreciated it. She hated to leave with the resolution so close, but what else could she do? She could not offer any further assistance, anyway; the authorities would take it from this point. As she rose to leave, Mr Gold took her hand and pressed it to his lips.

"My lady, I must also offer you some apologies. We wanted a quick and simple end to all this; and perhaps I was blind to things in my haste to bring a resolution to the matter. You must understand, of course, that here in the country, we are a tight knit community and we cannot allow the threat of the unknown, the uncertainty of a potential killer on the loose, to trouble the populace."

You don't want to risk upsetting the labour force, she thought, but she smiled politely. "I understand, sir," she assured him.

"You do?"

"Yes, although I do not agree with you," she added wickedly.

He sighed. "No, I suppose you don't. You are full of ideals. Women can be; you don't work in the world as we do, in the messy everyday of grey areas. You can have lofty ideas about right and wrong. That said, it is your guidance — women in general — that keep us men on the right path, is it not? And that is what I am thanking you for."

Smiling politely was becoming rather difficult. She hoped he stopped talking soon. She pulled on her gloves. "It has been my pleasure."

"Indeed. I think you are colouring the truth a little. Even so … your tenacity does you credit, my lady, and I wish you a prosperous career."

"Career?"

"Why, yes." Now it was his turn to smile wickedly. "It seems, with one thing and another, you have a talent here to stir up trouble, one might say. The world is changing fast, my lady, and the constables and the police cannot keep up. Now, of course, no lady can be involved in such dirty matters and yet … and yet…"

"A lady such as myself, who has left ladyship behind…"

"Indeed so. And it is that or marriage, and if I may be so frank, well…" But he was not able to be frank, and he stumbled to a halt.

She laughed, and adjusted her hat. "One last thing," she said. "What of the boy that set the fire at the mill?"

Mr Gold bristled at that. "Your brother-in-law has found a weak spot in his heart. The boy is to return to work there."

"How marvellous."

"Ha. And it will only take him seven years of wageless work to repay the debt. I'd have transported the little cur, for my part. But Mr Welsh is a high-minded man."

"And it is to his credit," she said, and sailed from the room.

* * *

Ruby was nearly smoking with rage that she had missed the conclusion, though as the journey progressed and she sunk deeper into the furs and blankets, she muttered long and low about how it was "no conclusion at all."

The trip south was slow and necessitated more than one overnight stop at inns along the way. A letter had been sent on ahead, and when they rolled into Clarfields on Christmas Eve, the household was ready for her. Quickly, the staff assembled on the front steps in the cold air and failing light. The warm yellow glow from the windows made them all smile. Cordelia roused herself and made sure to greet each person by name and to ask after personal details, but as quickly as she could, so that they could all get inside and back to the warmth.

And a letter had come that morning. Neville Fry, her

slender and high-voiced butler, brought the thick envelope to her on a silver tray as she sat in her drawing room by the fire. She was feeling hot and sweaty. She was used to dressing for her aunt's arctic premises and it was a shock to be in her own cosy place once more.

It was from the Justice, and she was delighted. For all his faults — of which she felt he had many — he had stayed true to his word, and had outlined in detail the events that had transpired after her departure.

She read it a few times, and drank a toast of red wine as she pondered.

Later, she summarised the contents of the letter to Ruby as her maid helped her to undress. Ruby was stroking the brush over Cordelia's unbound hair, and dotting it with powder from time to time.

"Mr Gold laid it out to Iris, just as I told him to do. That constable was there, also, and the newspaper man. She confessed, of course. I knew she would."

"How did you know?" Ruby said.

"I am a good judge of people."

Ruby's brush strokes barely faltered. Cordelia noticed, but said nothing. Ruby said, "Well, in some circumstances … aren't we all? Anyway. Well done, my lady. And what of Percy?"

"Sadly he, too, faces trial for the murder of the real

captain."

"Sadly?"

"He had a charm, a boyishness, did you not find?"

"I suppose so," Ruby said. "But I trusted him no further than John Kitt, in the end. Whatever did happen to him? Will they not investigate *his* murder? I am surprised at you, my lady, that you did not feel the need to discover his truth."

"I had enough to handle, and it was only the death of Lizzie that you asked me to look into."

"There is more to it than that, my lady," Ruby said.

Cordelia felt a little sick and light headed. *Had someone talked? Had someone seen what Geoffrey had done? Together, they were complicit…* Careful to sound casual, she said, "What, then?"

"Kitt was working against you and your class, my lady. You are probably relieved that he is gone, like all the rest of them."

"That is not true. I have read his pamphlets and he is right. Or at least, maybe the Chartists — the real ones — have some valid points. John Kitt was beyond all that, though, at the end. He had left their peaceful ideals behind."

"And you'd know because…?" There was a tartness to Ruby's voice.

"Ruby, I thought we were past this. Remember your

place."

Ruby began to bind up Cordelia's hair into a soft bun for the night, and she slipped a silk bonnet over her head to keep her tresses shiny and fuzz-free. "Even so," she said after a hesitation, "even so, my lady. I thought little of him, in the end, but he was a man with a soul like any other. No one cares for his death, do they?"

Cordelia looked at her maid's reflection in the mirror on the table before them. "Truly? I think you are correct. No one cares. And that is sad. But do you think that his actions were really helping the Chartists' cause?"

Ruby narrowed her eyes and did not reply. She gathered up the brushes and powders and began to tidy up.

"Exactly," Cordelia said. "He was going to do them harm, in the end. He was going to harm the Chartists' cause. Now, is all set for Christmas Day?"

"Well, I strayed into the kitchen and Mrs Unsworth threw a mince pie at me. I saw Stanley praying somewhere and later, he was scowling at the tree and saying it was pagan. Geoffrey is doing whatever he does, wherever he does it. So yes, everything seems normal."

"Excellent. And yourself?"

"Me, my lady?"

"Yes, you."

Ruby shrugged and turned away. "I am glad that you

did as you said you would, and found out the truth about Lizzie McNab," she said. "My lady ... thank you."

"Go now," Cordelia said. "The rest of the night is your own."

Ruby left. Cordelia felt the sudden emptiness of the room and she shivered. Hundreds of miles away, her aunt was relaxing in the peace of her own house; no companion, no seamstress, only her brother-in-law close by. Yet she was content with that.

Am I content? Cordelia thought.

I was. She stood up and moved away from the dressing table. *But I am rather enjoying being in the thick of things once more. After Christmastime, maybe sometime in the new year, perhaps I shall go to London. The ton shall not accept me, of course, yet there are those like me — on the edges of things — well, I rather think I can have some fun.*

Septimus Gibb, her agent, could open a few doors for her. Maybe she'd write that book after all.

She smiled at her reflection, and it cheered her that her reflection smiled back.

HISTORICAL NOTE

Chapter two - Our first introduction to the fictional John Kitt — he uses some words I have taken from a speech by the Chartist William Lovett which you can find here:

http://infed.org/archives/e-texts /william_lovett_on_education.htm

Chapter six - the Yorkshire Hussars (the volunteer yeomanry) did NOT assemble in 1845 but they did, indeed, assist at Cleckheaton riots and were raised in other places in 1842 against the possible rioters. Their uniforms changed over time but my descriptions are accurate for 1845. Full details here:

http://www.britishempire.co.uk/forces/armyunits/ yeomanry/yorkshirehussars.htm

Chapter ten — "Mr Greg's efforts in Cheshire" is a reference to Quarry Bank Mill at Styal and it is well worth a visit. It's National Trust property now. Back then, they really were seen as at the forefront of charitable endeavour … to our eyes, making children of ten years old work all day and then attend school doesn't seem so philanthropic. But against the working conditions of many others, this was a strange paradise indeed. At least they were allowed to see a doctor, and care was taken for their health — though that was more of a matter of protecting one's investment in the workforce, I'd imagine.

Thanks for reading! I'm an independent author. If you have the time, please do leave a review on Amazon. It makes a very real difference to an author's livelihood. Do note this book has been written in British English, which is just like American English but we like to use more vowels.

For news of future releases, why not sign up to my spam-free newsletter? Go here:

http://issybrooke.com/newsletter/

Look out for more adventures involving Cordelia and her retinue – coming throughout 2016.

Also available: contemporary light cozy mysteries set in Lincolnshire. The Some Very English Murders series is available here:

http://www.amazon.com/gp/product/B019U21S7C